"Samantha. I think maybe it's more than friendship on my end."

"It can't be, Harry. We can't let it be. Either of us. We're not ready for anything more."

Rather than respond, Harry got up and walked around the desk. He took her into his arms and gently, oh-so-tenderly kissed her. It was a soft kiss of introduction, growing bolder and decisive with every second—or was it minute?—it went on.

A small voice in Samantha's head said, *Pull away. Stop this now.*

But she didn't agree as she took control of the kiss, deepening it as she pressed into Harry's chest. She needed to be closer.

When they finally broke apart, she took an immediate step back.

"I think we both need to admit what we've been developing over the last few weeks is stronger than friendship." His voice sounded raspy. "There's friendship there, but that's not all...."

Dear Reader,

I have four kids, and I'll confess I've volunteered a lot at their grade school. I was the kindergarten story lady. I participated in Halloween parties, field trips and even the Christmas Fair. Maybe that's why I feel such a big connection to Samantha and her fellow social planning committee members, Michelle and Carly. But while the committee brought the three women together, what they discover is a true friendship. A friendship that helps all three women along the rocky road to rediscovering love.

It's been a year since Samantha's husband walked out and her world crumbled. Now she's feeling stronger and more optimistic. Despite a glass-half-full outlook, she's not sure she's ready to stumble again. But love isn't something you can plan on. It's a gift. And there's no denying it when it finds you. So when Harry, the new principal at school, calls her into his office, she finds more than she bargained for with the interim principal.

I hope you enjoy my first Harlequin American Romance novel—book one in my AMERICAN DADS trilogy. Come visit me at HollyJacobs.com and say hi! I love hearing from readers.

Holly

Once Upon
a Thanksgiving

HOLLY JACOBS

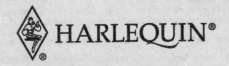

HARLEQUIN®

TORONTO • NEW YORK • LONDON
AMSTERDAM • PARIS • SYDNEY • HAMBURG
STOCKHOLM • ATHENS • TOKYO • MILAN • MADRID
PRAGUE • WARSAW • BUDAPEST • AUCKLAND

ISBN-13: 978-0-373-75236-2
ISBN-10:   0-373-75236-9

ONCE UPON A THANKSGIVING

ABOUT THE AUTHOR

In 2000 Holly Jacobs sold her first book to Harlequin Enterprises. She's since sold more than twenty novels to the publisher. Her romances have won numerous awards and made the Waldenbooks bestseller list. In 2005 Holly won a prestigious Career Achievement Award from *Romantic Times BOOKreviews*. In her nonwriting life, Holly is married to a police lieutenant and together they have four children. Visit Holly at www.HollyJacobs.com, or you can snail-mail her at P.O. Box 11102, Erie, PA 16514-1102.

Books by Holly Jacobs

HARLEQUIN EVERLASTING
17—THE HOUSE ON BRIAR HILL ROAD

SILHOUETTE ROMANCE
1557—DO YOU HEAR WHAT I HEAR?
1653—A DAY LATE AND A BRIDE SHORT
1683—DAD TODAY, GROOM TOMORROW
1733—BE MY BABY
1768—ONCE UPON A PRINCESS
1777—ONCE UPON A PRINCE
1785—ONCE UPON A KING
1825—HERE WITH ME

Don't miss any of our special offers. Write to us at the following address for information on our newest releases.

Harlequin Reader Service
U.S.: 3010 Walden Ave., P.O. Box 1325, Buffalo, NY 14269
Canadian: P.O. Box 609, Fort Erie, Ont. L2A 5X3

This is for everyone at St. John's School, especially the parents who have served on the PTA or volunteered in any way. Thanksgiving is a holiday where we give thanks, and I'm thankful to have been a part of such a great community for more than twenty years.

Prologue

Samantha Williams looked at the reflection in her bedroom mirror as she strained to button her jeans. She knew she needed to lose at least ten pounds, but starting up with the Women's Weight Center again didn't enthuse her. And she wanted to be enthused.

After the hardest year of her life, Samantha was determined to cultivate a more upbeat disposition. She'd picked up *How to Be Happy Without Really Trying* at the Borders Express in the Millcreek Mall last week. Step one on the path to happiness, as listed in the book, was to cultivate optimism. Well, she was going to be optimistic this week, even if it killed her.

Samantha adjusted her rose-colored glasses as she struggled with her jeans button. She could do this. She sucked in her stomach and tried the button again.

It slipped through the hole and Samantha felt a spurt of elation.

Okay, it was a small victory, but Samantha reveled in it, then released her breath and found that the small bit of stomach she referred to as her *baby-pooch* had oozed over the waistband.

For a moment, she began to slip off the positive-thinking bandwagon, but then she hoisted herself back up on it and sucked in her stomach. One bit of baby-pooch wasn't going to ruin her sunny disposition.

She'd just hold her stomach in today and maybe, if she made it an all-day project, her abs would get stronger without doing millions of crunches. And if her abs got stronger her baby-pooch would disappear, her clothes would fit better and she could skip Women's Weight Center meetings all together. And that would definitely make her happy.

Yes, there was an upside to everything. The kids had just started a new school year and she was going to make it a new start for herself, as well.

Her kids had all been lobbying for a dog. Maybe if she had a dog that had to be walked, she'd be more inclined to actually get out every day.

It couldn't hurt to go down to the pound and just take a look. The kids would love a dog. Of course, she wasn't sure if the cat would, but he'd adjust.

The phone rang, interrupting her dog thoughts.

She picked the receiver up off the nightstand. "Hello." She walked toward the kitchen, knowing the kids would be late for school if she didn't hurry them along. She had Tuesday mornings off, and after she ran them to their elementary school, she planned to spend the rest of her morning running all over Erie, Pennsylvania, doing the dozen errands on her list.

"Hi, Samantha, it's Heidi."

Samantha stopped dead in her tracks, and it had nothing to do with her daughter Stella's makeshift tent that was blocking her path.

Phone calls from the PTA president first thing in the morning did not bode well.

Be positive, she reminded herself. Heidi was a friend.

"Heidi, it's so good to hear from you." She smiled as

she said the words, hoping to infuse them with sunshine that she wasn't quite sure she felt.

Samantha climbed over the tent and into the kitchen as Heidi said, "We missed you at the PTA meeting last night. It was the first one of the year, and you know how important those meetings can be."

The remnants of the kids' breakfast lay scattered all over the island counter. Grunge, the cat, was licking a puddle of spilled milk off the floor. Samantha gently pushed the cat off the spot and started wiping the mess up. "Oh, I'm so sorry. I got home from a crazy day at work and PTA is normally the first Monday of the month, but that was last week and Labor Day. It never occurred to me that in September the meeting was the second Monday—" She stopped midwipe. She had a sneaking suspicion that there was more to this phone call than an early morning hello and update on the meeting. "Well, you don't want to hear my excuses for missing the meeting. Suffice to say, I'll be there next month for sure."

"About that, Samantha—"

Samantha dropped the sponge. She knew she was done for. "I know what happens when someone skips a meeting."

She remembered when Connie missed the April meeting last year. She was *volunteered* for the eighth-grade all-day bus trip to Toronto. To this day, Connie wouldn't speak about the trip. When asked, she turned pale, the tick near her left eye would start to jump and she'd change the subject. Occasionally she mumbled the word *coatroom,* but that was all.

Samantha just hoped there were no field trips scheduled this early in the year. "You might as well just tell me what job I've been assigned."

Maybe it was a fun job. Reading to kindergarten or

something. Or working a bake sale, which might not be good for her overflowing stomach, but was always a prime PTA job to snag.

Her attempts at positive thinking faded rapidly when Heidi didn't respond. "Heidi?"

"Well…"

Chapter One

Samantha Williams was a newly rehabilitated optimist. Since Tuesday's stomach sucking, she'd maintained her glass-half-full worldview.

Yet on days like today, she was reminded that half full was just as easily half empty. After all, Fridays should be spent joyfully anticipating the weekend with the kids. But when the kids' cat brought her a gift—a field mouse sort of gift—first thing in the morning, she should have guessed that the only thing she'd be anticipating was the day's end.

Still, she'd tried to continue her positive outlook. She'd firmly reminded herself that unlike other cats, Grunge never killed his *presents*. He only caught them and gave them. That was definitely a silver lining.

Also on the plus side, there was the fact that she'd chased Grunge's gift around the living room. Chasing a mouse might not sound positive, but she counted it as a cardio exercise, and added to the fact she'd been sucking in her stomach since Tuesday, she was way up on her physical exercise for the week.

Her boys—Stan, Seton and Shane—all helped her try to corner the terrified rodent, while her daughter Stella stood on the couch screaming directions when she wasn't just generally screaming. Uh, the good thing about that was...

Samantha was stumped and decided to count it as family time and that was always good, since the boys were thirteen, twelve and eleven, they were frequently more interested in hanging out with friends than with her. But it was hard to count chasing mice as a proper family activity, especially with eight-year-old Stella's shrieking.

Who knew that seeing the glass as half full was so much harder than seeing it as half empty?

Samantha had held off starting chapter two of *How to be Happy Without Really Trying.* She wanted to feel that she'd mastered chapter one's positive outlook first. And to that end, she'd asked, how could her day get worse than cardio mouse chasing?

And that one particular thought on her way into work was akin to throwing down a gauntlet and challenging the universe to step up its game. And man, what a game the universe had.

Dr. Jackson's pediatric office had been swamped with flu cases, and since it was only September, and way too early for the official start of the flu season, Samantha had been unprepared for the onslaught of patients. She loved being an RN, but some days she dreamed of doing something—almost anything—other than giving shots to terrified toddlers, holding screaming babies and comforting angst-ridden mothers. She tried to find something positive about the day's cases, but the best she could come up with was at least they weren't inundated with stomach viruses. It was lame, and she knew it, but she gave herself points anyway.

She'd finally admitted defeat when she received a phone call from the new principal asking for a meeting next week to discuss her sons. The kids were at their father's this weekend, so she wouldn't find out what happened until Sunday night when they got home. But she would find out. She'd learned, through her numerous trips to the principal's office last year, that forewarned was forearmed.

Yes, today might be Friday, but it had been the hands-down worst day of her week. And while she'd have loved nothing better than leaving work and heading home, the day wasn't quite over yet. She still had her first meeting with the committee she'd been *volunteered* for. A seven o'clock meeting on a Friday night seemed a rather stiff price to pay for missing one PTA meeting.

As she pulled up in front of Erie Elementary at six fifty-eight that evening, Samantha tried to muster any fleeting remnants of her rose-colored glasses. The best she could come up with was that no matter what happened at the meeting of the Social Planning Committee, she was on her way home afterward. That was definitely a good thing.

She turned off the car. Rather than get out, she sat in it a moment and just looked at the old brick school building, with its row of massive oaks in front of it and the smaller twin maples flanking the entry. The leaves on the trees were that tired green that meant they'd be changing into their fall colors soon. A few had fallen prematurely, and lay on the grass. And others had jumped the gun and started to hint at the oranges and reds they'd all be soon.

The sun was sinking low on the horizon, leaving the city in the pre-dusk gloom. It was getting dark earlier and earlier. Samantha loved the cool autumn nights. Technically, it might be late summer, but to Samantha, as soon as Labor Day had been celebrated, her autumn began.

She realized that she felt a bit more centered.

Coming back to the school was, in so many ways, like coming home.

Erie Elementary School was a small private grade school known for its strong academics and modest tuition.

Not much had changed about Erie Elementary since Samantha had attended the school... She did the math—could it really be twenty years since she'd graduated eighth grade?

She got out of her car and walked toward the main doorway.

Her mood lifted slightly. It wasn't quite back to her jean-buttoning high of Tuesday, but it was better than her principal's-on-the-phone low this afternoon.

Maybe this PTA committee wouldn't be so bad. How hard could planning a couple school functions be?

Samantha hurried inside, up a half set of steps, and across the hall to the meeting room.

"Hi, Carly. Michelle," she called out as cheerily as she could manage.

She knew the two other women on the committee in a peripheral way. They all had seventh graders. And even without that, Erie Elementary was small enough that everyone knew everyone else, even if only slightly. That was a big advantage. The school had that it-takes-a-village-to-raise-a-child sort of feel to it. The downside of belonging to a small school community was that it was similar to a small town—no one could sneeze without everyone else knowing about it.

Which is how Samantha knew Carly Lewis, a tiny, dark-haired woman who seemed to live life with a giant ferocity that Samantha admired. Carly was going through a messy divorce with her ex because she'd found him and his secretary together. Carly's kids, Sean and Rhiana, were only ten months apart, and both were in seventh grade with Samantha's son, Seton.

Michelle Hamilton was raising her nephew, Brandon,

who was also in Seton's class. Tall, blond and always organized, Michelle was PTA President Heidi's friend. To the best of Samantha's knowledge, there had never been anything about Michelle for the Erie Elementary gossips to sink their teeth into, other than the fact she'd been very young when her sister died and she'd taken her nephew into her home.

The two women were seated at one of the small round tables in the school's meeting room.

"Hi, Samantha. Have a seat." Michelle nodded at the chair across from her. "I brought refreshments." There was a small cooler of sodas and a foil-wrapped platter on the table.

"We were just going to open them." Carly peeled back the foil and exposed a tray of cookies.

Behave, Samantha warned herself, sucking her stomach in a bit farther as a reminder. She reached in the cooler and took a diet cola, while Carly and Michelle each took a napkin's worth of cookies.

"They look great," she assured Michelle, "but I'm stuffed. Maybe I'll have one later."

Michelle nodded, and rather than comment on Samantha's cookie-less status, asked, "So how are things?"

Just as Samantha knew about Carly's divorce, everyone at Erie Elementary knew that Phillip had walked out on her and they'd divorced. For more than a year, people's voices had gone soft when they asked about him, as if whispering the question would make Samantha's answer easier. She was equally sure the school was aware of how little Phillip had been involved with the kids since they split up.

Michelle's voice had that asking-about-your-ex tone to it. "Everything's great," Samantha replied in her most optimistic voice. "My ex has the kids this weekend, so I've got the night to myself."

She tried to sound enthused. And really, a night to herself was a treat. But she was worried about the kids. This was only the third time in a year that Phillip had taken all four of their kids. She could deal with him walking out on her. They'd married so young and people changed. Though it hurt at the time, she'd accepted they'd grown apart. But walking out on his kids? That was harder to forgive. She worried how, after such a long absence, Phillip was dealing with them.

She changed the subject. "So we're in charge of the PTA social events this year?"

"Yes. We're the official Social Planning Committee. Heidi gave me the files." Michelle reached into her briefcase and pulled out manila folders.

Carly grinned. "So, did you both join the committee on your own, or were you volunteered for missing the general PTA meeting, too?"

"Missed it," Samantha admitted and smiled, as well. "I should have known better. Remember Connie?"

Michelle nodded.

Carly grimaced.

"Michelle? Volunteer or volunteered?" Samantha quizzed. Both she and Carly looked at the cool blonde as they waited.

Samantha expected Michelle, who was always working on one committee or another, to say she'd volunteered, but for a moment Michelle's placid facade faded.

"I missed it, too," she confessed. Carly looked as surprised as Samantha felt. Michelle was not the type of woman who missed meetings. She was the type who probably had a color-coded calendar hanging in the kitchen, along with a PDA that kept her apprised of her schedule when she wasn't home.

"I was sick," Michelle explained, then added, "but I'd have probably volunteered if I'd been there, so it's no problem. At least it won't be if we divide the duties."

"What exactly are the Social Planning Committee's duties?" Carly asked, popping another cookie into her mouth.

Samantha's stomach growled, so she took a sip of her diet cola, and tried not to look at the biggest chocolate chip cookie in the center of the tray. It was calling to her like a siren singing for a passing ship. She sucked her stomach in again, and tried to focus her attention on Michelle.

"We plan all the PTA's major social events. The Thanksgiving Pageant, the Christmas Fair, the Valentine Dance and the end-of-year hoopla. Heidi had hoped to find a fourth member for the committee, that way each of us could assume the lead for one of the events, but…"

Michelle left the sentence hanging, and Carly filled in, laughing as she said, "But we were the only three moms who missed the first meeting?"

Michelle grinned ruefully. "That sums it up. And the parents who were there knew better than to volunteer. This is an all-year committee. Heidi said she'll continue to look for a fourth member, and if she can't find someone then she'll take over the end-of-year event herself. So that leaves the three of us with Thanksgiving, Christmas and Valentine's Day. I've given this some thought…" She paused. "Samantha, you have Stella in third grade, right?"

Samantha nodded.

"That's what I thought. The third-graders tradition-ally put on the Thanksgiving Pageant. They're old enough to learn the lines, and young enough to be cute, prancing around as turkeys and pumpkin pies."

"Yeah, can you imagine seventh-graders doing it?" Carly asked.

They all laughed, then Michelle continued, "Well, it seems logical for you to take the Thanksgiving Pageant because of Stella, if that's okay? And then…"

Michelle was an accountant, or belonged to some other such number-crunching profession that required organization, which might explain the folder with its papers, breaking the three events down, assigning Samantha point for Thanksgiving, Michelle for Christmas, and Carly for Valentine's Day.

They'd both accepted Michelle as the head of the committee without a vote or even discussion, but as far as Samantha was concerned, that was fine. Whatever activity she was in charge of was pretty much the same. And because she was responsible for the first of the events, she'd be done sooner rather than later.

Maybe it was time to read the next chapter in *How to be Happy Without Really Trying,* because she was pretty sure she was getting the optimism chapter down to a science.

Michelle handed Samantha and Carly notes from the previous social committees. "I think by making one of us the leader for each of the activities, and the other two just providing backup, things shouldn't be too tough. Does that work for both of you?" Michelle asked, her hands neatly folded on top of her file.

Carly had just eaten another cookie, and Samantha was desperately trying not to notice the look of utter contentment the woman obviously felt as she chewed the hundred-plus calories. Since Carly's cookie-stuffed mouth precluded her answering, Samantha replied for the both of them. "It all sounds good."

"Great." Michelle slipped her folder back into her

bag. "Why don't we plan on meeting every other week? Unless babysitters are a problem for you, Samantha?" Samantha knew both Michelle and Carly had seventh graders, so babysitting wasn't too much of a worry because they were old enough to be on their own for a few hours. Things were harder with four kids, especially when her baby was only eight.

"Now that Stan's in eighth grade, I've been letting him babysit for short spurts, and so far he's done fine." She knocked on wood, which made Michelle and Carly grin.

"It's only been a year that I've let Sean and Rhiana stay home without a babysitter. It's hard to let go, but I'm bound and determined they learn to stand on their own two feet." There was a quiet determination in Carly's expression. Samantha wondered if Carly's ex had something to do with that.

Michelle smiled. "Okay. Then, same time, same place in two weeks. Samantha, in the meantime, you can read last year's pageant notes, and see what you need from Carly and me."

Samantha nodded. It was clear the business portion of the meeting was over.

The chocolate chip cookies were still there, beckoning her, and since *positive* was her new watchword, Sam decided that she was *positive* she'd be happier with that chocolate chip cookie than with just the diet cola.

Cookie in hand, she did indeed feel happier as she turned to Michelle and Carly. "Have either of you met the new principal? I have an appointment with him on Monday."

She took a bite of the cookie and admitted she'd been wrong—this wasn't mere happiness, it was nirvana. "This is amazing."

If she'd written the book, she'd have definitely

included a chapter on chocolate chip cookies being the key to earthly contentment.

"Glad you like it," Michelle said. "And I haven't met Mr. Remington yet and I don't know much. Heidi told me that he was at the first PTA meeting, but we all missed that." She grinned ruefully. "Heidi liked him. I guess he's some kind of interim principal. An old friend of Geri Flamini, the superintendent. He was in town taking some graduate classes, and when Principal Tooly quit so abruptly. Anyway, Geri asked him to fill in at Erie Elementary until she can find a permanent replacement. So he's just here until sometime in December, unless she finds the replacement faster."

"What was he doing before working here?" Carly asked.

"Working as assistant principal somewhere in Ohio," Heidi said. "He's on sabbatical while he finishes his Master of Administration here in the area. I'm not sure which college. He'll be finished in December and then is going back to Ohio, back to his school."

"Michelle, if that's not knowing much, I'd love to listen to you talk about something you know a lot about," Samantha teased.

"Well, according to my kids, this Mr. Remington is better than Tooly. Although, that's not saying much," Carly added. "I'm not principal material by any stretch of the imagination, and I'd have done a better job than Tooly did."

Samantha's boys had a difficult time with their dad's leaving. Their difficulty was reflected in their attitude at school, which meant frequent trips to the principal's office. Principal Tooly had been the bane of Samantha's existence, and it was nice to hear that her opinion of him wasn't simply colored by her kids' experiences.

"I saw more of Mr. Tooly last year than anyone but his wife should have had to," Samantha admitted. Tooly had tried to corral her boys with an iron fist. His method only seemed to make matters worse.

With a new principal on board—even if he was only an interim one—Samantha was hopeful that this would be a better year than last year. The boys had finally seemed to adjust to her divorce from Phillip, and his taking them this weekend was a good sign that he was going to be more active in their lives.

She slipped on her newly polished rose-colored glasses.

Michelle passed Samantha another chocolate chip cookie, and since it seemed rude not to take it, she did and felt a keen sense of satisfaction. Maybe that was the trick—appreciate the chocolate chips while you can because you never knew when the cat would bring you another mouse.

Michelle shrugged. "Sorry, we're not much help about Principal Remington. You'll have to fill us in at our next meeting."

They visited awhile longer, bragging about their kids and just chatting about this and that.

Somewhere in the midst of the conversation, Samantha realized she'd missed hanging out with other women. Over the last year, she'd been so busy with the kids, with just getting through her divorce and the aftermath, that she hadn't kept up with her friends.

"Oh, my it's almost eight-thirty." Michelle studied her watch. "I can't believe we've been here this whole time."

"And eating cookies," Samantha added. "I can't remember when I had cookies that good. Of course, I'm going to have to suck my stomach in for the next month to make up for all I ate."

"Suck your stomach in?" Carly asked.

"It's my new form or exercise." Samantha outlined

her alternative to crunches and joined in when Carly and Michelle both chuckled.

"Maybe I'll try it," Carly said. "I know I need to exercise now that I'm in my thirties—my very early thirties," she clarified with a grin.

"They say thirty is the new twenty, and if that's the case, it makes you practically in your teens," Samantha teased Michelle, who was barely in her late twenties, tops. Seton had been in third grade when Michelle's nephew, Brandon, had joined the class. Samantha remembered hearing at the time that Brandon's mother, Michelle's sister, had died. The first time she'd seen Michelle at a school function, she'd been struck by how young the girl was to be taking on the responsibility of an eight-year-old.

"My nephew Brandon has been doing his best to prematurely age me, if that makes you feel better."

Samantha laughed and put an arm around Michelle's shoulder.

They gathered up their things, and Samantha carried Michelle's cooler for her as they made their way out of the school, turning lights out as they went. Michelle had the PTA's set of keys, and locked the school's door after them, then took the cooler. "I know this was a working meeting, but it was fun."

"It was. Next time I'll bring the snack," Carly offered.

"I'm looking forward to it," Samantha replied and they all waved and went to their cars.

Samantha felt better than she had in a long time despite her marathonish Friday.

Maybe Heidi had done her a favor volunteering her for this committee…?

Just then her cell phone rang, and her ex's home number was flashing on the screen. "Hello."

"Mom, it's Stan," her oldest said, as if she wouldn't recognize his voice.

"How are things at your dad's?" This wasn't just the first time he'd taken the kids in more than three months, it was the first time the kids had spent the night at Phillip's new place.

"Fine," came Stan's monosyllabic response.

It was enough to tell her that something was up. "But…?" she prompted. "It's fine, but…?"

"Stella hid Grunge in her bag. Dad wasn't happy, and uh…"

Stella shrieked in the background.

A spurt of fear had Sam mentally calculating the quickest route to Phillip's place. "What's the matter?"

"Grunge doesn't like Dad's new puppy. He's got him cornered under the bed, and Stella's afraid Grunge's going to get hurt. She's the only one worried about the cat. The rest of us are worried about the puppy. Dad wants to know if you'd come get Grunge?"

"Tell him I'll be there in a few minutes."

Retrieving the cat hadn't been part of her evening's plans, but Samantha couldn't help but be glad she'd have a chance to tell the kids good-night.

Her kids kept life interesting.

Samantha Williams was positive about that.

Chapter Two

On Monday, Harry Remington looked at the dark-haired woman sitting outside his office. She was wearing a set of hospital scrubs. "Mrs. Williams?"

The woman nodded, then stood. She didn't quite reach Harry's shoulder, which meant she looked up at him, and as she did, he couldn't help but notice her eyes were a warm brown. He wondered if they crinkled when she smiled. They looked as if they might. He couldn't be sure though, because right now she was definitely not smiling.

As a matter of fact, she was looking at him with a mixture of curiosity and antipathy. Maybe if she wasn't fond of principals in general—having read her boys' files, he could understand why her dealings with the previous principal might have colored her opinion. Or maybe something about him in particular had made her wary.

So he smiled his best I'm-here-to-help smile to put her at ease.

She extended her hand. "It's *Ms*. Williams. Samantha, actually. You must be our new interim principal, Mr. Remington?"

They shook hands. Her grip was firm as she assessed him.

"Harris Remington. Harry to my friends."

There was a look of surprise as he said his name, then she studied him even closer than she had before. He couldn't figure out what she saw. Her expression didn't offer any clue. "Let's go into my office and talk."

Harry led Mrs. Williams—*Ms. Williams, Samantha, actually,* he corrected himself—into his office, trying not to notice how unsettled the room still felt. Granted, he'd only be here at Erie Elementary until December, but the office's current state of chaos wasn't like him.

Harry had taken a sabbatical for the term from his school in Columbus, planning to have some downtime in Erie while he finished his graduate degree in Education Administration, which was a requirement if he wanted to become a principal.

But instead of the calm term he'd envisioned, his old friend Geri had called asking him to take the job at Erie Elementary until she could find a permanent replacement. So, Harry had hit the ground running, and had been so busy with the start of the school year, and becoming familiar with the kids and teachers, as well as starting his evening classes at Edinboro University, that he hadn't finished unpacking his office boxes.

"I love what you've done with the place," she teased, a smile playing lightly on her lips as she took in the disheveled-looking room. Then, as if realizing she was fraternizing with the enemy, her expression became serious. "Sorry. That was totally inappropriate. We're here to talk about the boys."

Harry had been on the verge of laughing, but at her abrupt change in demeanor, he didn't. He simply indicated a chair across from his. "It wasn't inappropriate. It was truthful and funny," he responded. She didn't lose her wary look. He gave up putting her at ease. It obviously wasn't going to happen. "Down to business then. Yes. About your boys and last week's food-fight incident."

She sighed, her expression becoming almost grim. "I know. When they got home from their dad's on Sunday they told me everything about the food fight on Friday. And I'll be frank, it's not much of a food fight when it's just my three boys. Seton and Shane didn't throw anything, they just got Stan to sit on his Little Debbie. But I read them the riot act. Seton and Shane will be paying for Stan's new school pants and Stan will pay for their shirts. He shouldn't have taken the chocolate he'd sat on to smear on them. The chocolate wouldn't come out of any of the clothes."

"They told you?" That was a surprise. Most kids tried to hide their misdeeds from their parents.

"They learned last year it's better to fess up than let me get blindsided when I come into the principal's office. And if you've looked at their files, you know they've had a lot of experience at confessing. That's the one good thing about my boys. They might make mistakes, but they always own up to them, and they never repeat the same mistake twice."

"I did notice that as I read over Principal Tooly's rather copious notes." For a moment, Harry thought she might offer up some explanation or excuse for the boys. He hoped she would give him a clue as to why they were acting out. But she merely sat there, waiting.

"Did any of Principal Tooly's punishments prove helpful, in your opinion?" he asked.

The question appeared to surprise her. Her eyes widened slightly and she cocked her head to one side, looking as if she were mulling his question over.

After a second or two, she straightened her head and shook it. "No, I wouldn't say any of Tooly's punishments were overly successful in dissuading my boys from their escapades. As a matter of fact, his punishments seemed to inspire even more practical jokes, many of which were directed at him."

"The school newsletter," Harry supplied, remembering the long diatribe of the previous principal. Mr. Tooly had gone on and on about the mock newsletter the boys had printed and delivered to every student at Erie Elementary. A mock newsletter that featured an in-depth article on Tooly. Some of the facts that the faculty assumed were false turned out to be otherwise. The one about Tooly's little gambling problem being one of the *otherwise* facts.

"Well, they did get an awful lot of the story right, which is why Mr. Tooly eventually lost his position. So that means you sort of owe my boys for your new job, even if it's only an interim one…right?" She offered him a weak smile.

Harry smiled back as he nodded. "There's a logic to that. But be that as it may, we have to do something about last week's prank. Does grounding them help?"

She shook her head.

"Then I suggest the two of us have to find a more creative way of convincing your sons that rules are there for a reason."

Again, she looked surprised. "What do you suggest? I know Tooly's preferred creative method would require shackles or ropes at best."

"No. I'm not a shackle man. I thought, for starters, what if they contribute to improving the school, more specifically, they come in on Saturday and help me paint the office and unpack my stuff?"

"Really? You're going to let the boys use paint…on purpose?" Samantha Williams didn't look as if she thought that was a good idea.

"Well, their graffiti last year convinced the art teacher

your sons had more than a degree of talent, and since detentions don't seem to work, maybe being forced to spend a day with their principal, helping with my work, might act as a deterrent."

"But they won't be just spending the day with you. They'll be spending a day with paint and all manner of ways to wreak havoc on a rather deserted school."

"Do you have a better suggestion?" he asked.

She seemed to think a moment, then shook her head. "No."

"Then let's give mine a try."

"You're sure you're up to three boys and painting supplies?"

Harry nodded, feeling a bit less sure than he was pretending to be in the face of her doubt.

"Well, then, all right. Uh, are you sure you don't want to yell at me about how parents today don't understand the definition of the word *discipline,* and tell me how in your day your parents made you go out to the willow tree in the backyard and cut a switch before I go? That was Tooly's favorite parting refrain."

He laughed. "My parents were pacifists through and through. No matter what kind of hijinks I came up with when I was young, they never spanked me. They were united in their attempts to tame me, but there was no physical punishment, so I guess I grew up without that kind of bloodlust." Harry's parents' marriage ended abruptly the year he entered seventh grade when they'd divorced. He'd asked around and learned Samantha and her husband divorced last year. Maybe that's why he felt so much empathy for her boys.

"I did manage my share of trouble," he assured Ms. Williams, "a lot of which happened right here at Erie Elementary."

"Harry…Harry Remington?" Ms. Williams mused. "When you introduced yourself I thought it might be the same Harry that was in Miss Ross's seventh-grade class."

He must have looked confused because she smiled and added, "I was Samantha Burger then, in Miss Wagner's fifth grade."

Sami Burger? Harry remembered a girl with absurdly long hair that she wore in two dark braids. "Sami?"

"It's Samantha these days, or even Sam. Only my mom calls me Sami, and only when she's trying to put me in my place."

For the first time, her expression was genuinely warm. "Welcome home, Harry. You moved away right after that, didn't you?"

"Right about that time. Mom and I went to stay with my grandparents in Ohio, so there would be someone to watch me while she went back to work."

This happened a month after his father had packed a moving van and left their house on Marvin Avenue. Harry remembered that the drive to Columbus lasted forever. In retrospect, he knew it was only a little more than four hours, but for a twelve-year-old boy who was leaving the only home he'd ever known, that drive had gone on interminably.

"I'm sorry we met again because of the boys misbehaving," she said, deftly bringing their conversation back to the matter at hand.

"I've gone through their files and it seems their problems started last year. They'd never been to the principal's office before that."

"My husband left us. Not just me, *us.* All of us. It's taken its toll on the kids, the boys especially. I think Stella's so young it hasn't hit her as hard, or maybe it's that they're boys and need their father and feel the lack more intensely.

I don't know. But you're right, their frequent visits to the principal's office started after he left."

"I'd like to suggest something. Some parents take offense, but…" He paused. "I could have our school counselor talk to them. We have one who rotates in, one day a week. It might help to hear someone else say it's not their fault. I'm not saying you haven't handled it well, or that—"

She smiled as she interrupted him. "Harry, I'm not a parent who takes offense when someone truly wants to help my boys. Principal Tooly didn't care *why* the boys were acting up in school and accused me of making excuses if I tried to explain. Maybe I was making excuses, but losing your father is a pretty good excuse, in my opinion."

Harry nodded, knowing the truth of that statement better than Samantha could understand. "Yes, it is, but we do have to try to stem the tide. So you don't mind if they talk to the counselor?"

"That would be great. I want to help them through this. I can love them and set firm rules, but I can't make their dad come back to us. I can't even get him to agree to regular visitation. Last weekend was the first time he'd seen them in months."

"I'm sorry, Sami…Samantha. Sorry for you, for them. Relationships are hel—" He searched for a more diplomatic word and finally said, "Hard."

"Bad breakup, too?" she asked.

"We're not here to talk about me, but rather your boys." He wanted to kick himself for the abruptness of his response because Samantha's expression became guarded again. "Sorry. It was bad and I'm obviously still not quite over it."

She accepted his apology with a nod. "Relationships

aren't just hard, they're hell." She stood. "It was nice seeing you again, Harry. I'm glad you're here at Erie Elementary."

He stood, as well. "At least until December. So we're on for Saturday, painting my office? Drop them off about eight?"

"I'm willing to try anything that will get them to toe the line. They'll be here, with painting clothes on. I just hope you know what you're doing."

"So do I," he said with a laugh.

She started toward the door, then stopped and turned around. "Thanks for taking the time to try to understand why the boys have had some problems, rather than just throwing the book at them."

"That's my job, Sami. Hopefully, with the two of us working together on this, we can help the boys find their way."

"I'd like that. I really would. It breaks my heart seeing them suffer because Phillip and I couldn't make a go of it. I've reassured them that both of us still love them, even if their father and I don't love each other anymore. But the fact their father's all but disappeared from their lives makes it hard for them to believe any of it."

"Even if he was around every day, it would still be hard. Kids are… What's a good word?" He paused and searched for the right description. "Self-centered maybe? They're so busy growing up, so focused on themselves, that they see the world as it affects them and they tend to personally claim all the credit or the blame. Your husband leaving has devastated them, and I'm sure they feel, no matter what you say, that his going was their fault. Maybe with a few other adults letting them know that it wasn't, they'll finally start to believe it. It just might take a while."

Harry knew it had taken a long time for him to get over feeling guilty about his parents' breakup. But eventually he did. It helped that both his mom and dad had gone on to find new, very happy relationships, and that they'd eventually become friends.

"And maybe if the boys can learn to believe it wasn't their fault their behavior at school will improve?"

Harry nodded. "We can hope." He reached out and put his hand on her shoulder…just the smallest gesture of comfort.

She seemed startled by his touch and froze for a moment. He dropped his hand, and she seemed to give herself a small shake, then as if nothing had happened said, "Thank you for really caring about my boys, Harry."

"My pleasure. Remember, I'm here, anytime if you need me."

"Thanks. It really was good seeing you again. You were a hero to all us younger kids. That time you put For Sale signs on all the teachers' lawns…" She chuckled.

"I think it would be a good idea if you kept my old escapades between you and me. I can't imagine hearing about that one would endear the new principal to any of the teachers."

"And my boys don't need any new ideas. You could give them a lot." She glanced at her watch. "I'd better run. I've got to meet with Mrs. Tarbot about the Thanksgiving Pageant, then I have to get back to work."

"Thanks for coming in, Sami."

"Thank you." She hurried down the hall.

Harry watched her head for the third-graders' classroom. Little Sami Burger. Samantha Williams.

She'd certainly grown up well.

The thought surprised him. It was the first time in months that he'd looked at a woman with that kind of appreciation. Since his breakup last spring, he hadn't even thought about dating. But looking at Samantha Williams, the idea was appealing.

He was only here for a few months while he finished his degree. This interim job was actually a godsend because it didn't leave him time to think about the past. There wasn't time to second-guess his decisions.

The move was obviously the right one, if he was thinking about asking a woman out. As long as both he and Samantha were clear that he was only here until the end of the year, there couldn't be any harm.

Maybe he'd ask her Saturday, after he spent the morning with her boys.

He looked around the office.

Yes, he couldn't wait until Saturday. He suspected it had less to do with getting his office in order, and more to do with seeing Sami Burger again.

SAMANTHA CHECKED HER watch that Saturday and realized it was ten to one. "Ready to pick up the boys, Stella?"

Stella was engrossed in some television show. Samantha knew it was rare that her youngest had the TV to herself. Generally the three boys, so close in ages and tastes, banded together and out-voted Stella's viewing choices.

Eight years old and gangly, with two long braids draped down her back, Stella was cuddled with Grunge in one of the recliners. "Do we have to go right now? The show's over in ten minutes."

"We can wait that long, but you're going to have to hurry up and get ready if we want to be there in time. And I'm pretty sure after a morning with the boys, Principal Remington will appreciate us not being late."

"Okay."

Samantha had spent her week trying to analyze what had happened in Harry's office when he touched her. It was a friendly pat on the shoulder, meant to be comforting. She knew that. But her reaction to it had been anything but comforting. It had disturbed her.

When Harry touched her she felt... She simply felt.

That's as close to an explanation as she'd come.

It was as if since Phillip left her, she'd shut down. Maybe it was even longer than that. She'd funneled everything into her kids, into work. She'd tried to forget that there was more.

That one touch reminded her.

She realized she was standing in the living room, ruminating again.

Whatever Harry's friendly gesture had awakened in her, it could simply go back to sleep, because Samantha didn't have time for it.

She pushed away the thought, and concentrated on all she had to do. In the kitchen, she finished putting away the last of the groceries. Every other weekend, she worked Saturday mornings at the office. This was one of her weekends off. And since the boys were occupied, she'd hurried and got as many of her chores done first, so she could take the rest of the time this afternoon and relax with the kids, guilt free.

She did a 360.

Everything was finished in the kitchen, so Samantha dashed down to the basement, threw the wet clothes into the drier, started another load in the washer, and on her way upstairs, grabbed a can of cat food from the shelf.

She set Grunge's dinner on the counter, and called, "Stella?"

"Coming." Her daughter sprinted into the kitchen,

Grunge still in her arms. "Can Grunge come pick up the boys? He likes going for rides."

Having experienced the cat in the car before, Samantha wasn't sure *likes* was the correct word. *Abhors* seemed closer to the mark. Rather than trying to reason with Stella, she simply said, "No. Remember what happened last week when you took him to your father's?"

"Dad's new dog is mean, and so's Lois." Stella dropped the cat and clapped a hand over her mouth.

It didn't take a detective to immediately realize that Stella had been told not to mention Lois, which meant that Lois was the new woman in Phillip's life.

"Honey, it's okay. You're not supposed to keep secrets from your mother. Not ever."

"Daddy said you might be sad if you knew he had a roommate."

Lois was living with Phillip? That's why he finally moved out of an apartment and into a house?

Sam waited for the pain of knowing she'd been replaced.

And waited.

And waited.

It didn't come.

She'd known that Phillip had dated during the last year. *Supposed* mutual friends felt it their duty to keep her informed on all his activities no matter how many times Samantha told them she didn't want to know.

Phillip had made his position perfectly clear when, bags in hand, he told her it was over, that there was no hope of reconciliation. The declaration had taken Samantha by complete surprise. She'd known things were bad, but not that bad.

In retrospect, she should have.

Phillip had spent six months prior to leaving

spending more and more nights working overtime at the office. Frequently sleeping there.

Yes, she'd seen the writing on the wall. She'd even suggested marriage counseling, but he'd been adamantly opposed. So his request for a quick divorce shouldn't have been a shock, but it had been. Now, a year later, the news that he was living with another woman wasn't.

When Phillip had left, she hadn't thought she'd ever recover, but she had. Well, mostly.

"Stella, honey, you can always tell me anything. Even if it might hurt me, you should tell me. Understand?"

"That's what Lois said to Daddy. That I couldn't keep his secrets from you."

"Well, Lois sounds like a very smart lady. I hope she makes your daddy happy. Speaking of happy, I think the boys'll be happy to see us. Let's go."

"The principal probably spent all day yelling at them." There was a combination of pity and sisterly glee at the thought of someone yelling at her brothers.

"I'm sure he didn't yell at them. Mr. Remington doesn't strike me as a yeller."

Stella gave her mother a look that said she didn't quite believe her. "But Mom, it's the boys."

Rather than debate the yellability of Stella's brothers with her, Samantha loaded her daughter, sans the cat, into the car. They drove the five minutes to Erie Elementary.

Samantha expected to see her three paint-spattered sons waiting on the steps. Instead, she found Stan, Seton and Shane playing a game of basketball with Harry, all of them sweaty looking, despite the mere sixty-degree day.

Momentarily, she flashed to that smallest of gestures, that pat on her shoulder Harry had given her.

The feeling of awakening she'd had then jumped again. This was ridiculous. Samantha ignored the feeling and focused on her sons.

At first, she thought it was three against one, but then she saw that Shane was on Harry's team and enjoying the fact that for once he had an advantage over his two older brothers.

Harry passed the ball to Shane, then blocked both Stan and Seton while Shane made the basket.

Samantha starting clapping while Stella whooped her delight.

Harry and the boys hurried over, sweaty and smiling.

"So is the office done?" Samantha asked.

The boys started talking over one another. She caught bits and pieces of their sentences. "Brown paint…"

"Boxes…"

"Nailing…"

"Want to see?" Harry asked.

"Sure," Samantha agreed and looked at her kids, expecting them to come along and show her their morning's work.

"We did it, so we've already seen it," Stan said. "We're gonna play some more ball." Before she could ask, he added, "Me and Stella against Shane and Seton."

Samantha found herself following Harry into the dark, quiet school. "So, really, how'd it go?"

He raked a hand through his hair, making it stand up a bit, reminding her of when he was younger and hadn't learned to tame his thick wild brown mane yet. "They were great. A huge help."

"Really?" She caught the tone in her voice and hastened to add, "It's not that I doubt my kids are great, but I'm biased. And to be honest, I've never had anyone in charge of a detention tell me they were great.

As a matter of fact, they have a whole different definition for my boys."

"There's a first for everything, and mine was an accurate description."

His office door was open. She smelled the clean, sweet scent of paint before she saw the results.

"Oh, wow, Harry, it's wonderful." She stood a moment and took it all in.

The walls were a rich brown, the shelves were filled with books and mementoes. There were even pictures and certificates on the wall. "How did you manage to hang those already?"

"We went with a quick-drying paint and that was our first project. Then we unpacked boxes, and by the time we were done, the paint was dry enough to hang the pictures."

"Oh. It doesn't look like the same office I saw on Tuesday. It suits you now."

It did. The warm, earthy tone fit Harry to a T. Speaking of fitting to Ts, Harry's T-shirt, which proudly proclaimed Principal…A Prince of a Pal, and showed a balding, crown-wearing cartoon figure carrying a school book, fit him in such a way that left Samantha with little doubt that Harry spent time at the gym.

A lot of time.

Her throat felt a bit dry and she swallowed convulsively.

Harry caught her looking at his now paint-splattered T-shirt. "A gift."

It took her a minute to realize he was referring to the T-shirt. She nodded, not sure what to say.

Harry waited a moment, and obviously assumed the nod would be her only response. "And you're right. I definitely feel more comfortable in a well-ordered space. The boys were a big help."

Samantha felt as if she'd recovered some of her wits, but was careful not to look at his chest. Instead, she spun a bit and said, "I'm glad it went well. They looked like they enjoyed this detention. You better be careful of that."

"They miss your husband. They talked a lot about seeing him last weekend."

She knew her kids were hurting, just as she knew there wasn't anything she could do about it, other than keep encouraging Phillip to take some interest.

"I wasn't prying," he assured her.

She looked up. "I didn't think you were. I appreciate that you listened to them. It's something Tooly never did."

"Well, I hope you appreciate it enough to overlook the fact I've invited the boys, invited all of you, out to lunch."

"Oh, Harry, you don't have to do—"

"Sami, the boys worked their butts off. This was more than just sitting in a classroom for an hour and doing some homework. They really worked. I want to say thank you. And everyone knows that pizza tastes better with company."

"Do they now?" she asked with a smile.

"Have you ever had a solo pizza?" He grimaced. "I don't recommend it."

"I have four kids, remember? I don't get many solo meals. But if I do get one, I'll bear your warning in mind and make sure it's not pizza." She stopped teasing and added, "If you're sure, then we'd be delighted to have lunch with you."

"I'm sure."

They walked back out of the school, and Harry threw the security switch, then closed and locked the door.

"Hey, Mom," Shane called, "Mr. Rem said he'd take us out for lunch, but only if it's okay with you."

Mr. Rem. She glanced at Harry. The name suited

him as well as the newly decorated office. She looked back at the kids. They'd stopped their game and waited, watching her. She could see how much they wanted to go, and even if she hadn't already said yes, she'd have agreed. "He already asked and I already said yes."

The boys whooped, and Stella just smiled.

"Shall we?" Harry asked.

"Sure." Samantha felt a bit first-date giddy, which was ridiculous since this was anything but a date. This was just Harry being nice. Nothing more. Nothing less.

HARRY COULDN'T REMEMBER the last time he'd had so much fun. Well, he could, but remembering hurt so much, he promptly tried to forget and simply concentrate on Sami Burger—no, Williams—and her kids. They'd opted to go to Patti's Pizza, which was just a couple minutes from the school. It was still at 38th and Pine, though it had moved to a new building across from where it had stood when he was young.

That's what coming home to Erie was like. Things were the same…except for the differences.

Buildings that had been renovated, businesses that had moved. Streets that had fallen into inner-city malaise, areas that were on an upswing.

Most were small changes, but that aside, Erie was still the same small town disguised as one of Pennsylvania's four largest cities.

"Earth calling Harry," Samantha said.

"Sorry. I was drifting. Remembering when I was a kid and we'd order pizzas here."

"Wow, Patti's is that old, Mr. Rem?" Stan asked, grinning.

"Watch it, boy," Harry replied with mock sternness.

All four of the kids laughed, which made Samantha smile.

Harry liked how the expression wasn't just in her lips. No, it sort of took over Samantha's whole face, especially around the eyes. He'd been right that first day when he thought her eyes would crinkle when she smiled or laughed. They did.

Seton looked more like his mother than Stan and Shane did. It was the wave in the boy's hair. The other two wore their hair cropped and straight. Harry wondered if Stan and Shane looked more like their father. On the heels of that thought, he wondered how the man could have ignored his kids for more than a year.

Stan was still chuckling over Harry's Patti's-being-that-old quip.

"Yes, Patti's was here when I was a kid, although it used to be across the street next to Burhenn's Pharmacy, Colonial Bakery and Paul Bunyan's Groceries. The old building didn't have any tables. Everything was to go."

"I like eating inside. I like how it smells in here," Stella added quietly. "Like Mommy's kitchen."

"You bake?" Harry asked.

"When I have time. Nothing fancy," she hastened to add. "Just plain kid-friendly stuff."

"Mommy makes the best chocolate chip cookies ever," Stella said.

Not to be outdone, Seton added, "And homemade macaroni and cheese. It's really cheesy."

"And pumpkin pies," Shane added. "I mean, you've never had pies like Mom's."

"I don't think I've ever had a homemade pie, except in a restaurant, and then it's restaurant-made, not really homemade." Harry cast his most practiced pathetic look toward Samantha.

"Was that a subtle hint?" she asked right on cue.

"Gee, you thought that was subtle? I'm going to have to work on the blatant part. I was just thinking, next time you made a pie, I wouldn't be averse to a piece."

"Mom always makes a big meal on Sunday," Seton said. "We help."

"I set the table and stir things," Stella told him.

"Maybe you could come?" Shane asked.

"I would never be rude enough to invite myself." Again, he gave Samantha his look.

She sighed and looked as put upon as she could manage, but Harry caught the twinkle in her eye that said she was teasing. "Harry, would you like to have dinner with us tomorrow? It's just meat loaf."

"And Mom will make pumpkin pie, right, Mom?" Seton said.

"I guess I could be convinced."

"Well, how could I say no to such an unexpected, unprompted, totally impromptu invitation?" He paused a fraction of a second, then added, "What time?"

"Noonish. We eat about one—"

"Then everyone has to *farm* for themselves the rest of the day," Stella proclaimed.

"That's fend," Seton said with seventh-grade disgust.

"Seton, I don't correct you like that," Samantha said gently.

Harry thought Seton might argue, but he looked at his mother's expression and sighed. "Sorry, squirt."

"Fend," Stella politely repeated.

Harry knew he should feel rather embarrassed by the blatancy of his fishing for a dinner invitation, but he couldn't quite manage it. All he felt was happy that he'd be spending the next day with Samantha and her kids.

He sat back and enjoyed the pizza. He looked from

one person to the next, and knew that this was what he'd always wanted. A big family where everyone talked over one another as they laughed and ate. Small squabbles popped up, but Harry didn't even mind them. That was part of being a family. Something he'd always felt he'd missed.

It wasn't that he didn't have a family. He loved his mother and father. But after they'd divorced, they'd both gone on with their lives and built new families. Families he'd never truly felt a part of.

For seven years he thought he'd build his own family with Teresa, but...

He shook off the sad thoughts and tried to concentrate on what was in front of him, rather than what he'd left behind. He sat back and allowed himself to enjoy this moment.

The only fly in the ointment—well, pizza—was Stan. The eighth-grader had started shooting Harry dark looks right after Samantha had invited Harry to dinner. Stan obviously wasn't pleased at the idea of his principal coming to his house, but the younger kids didn't seem to mind. Harry wondered if he should back out, yet in the end, he couldn't bring himself to. He really wanted to spend more time with the Williams family.

More specifically, Samantha Williams.

He remembered her as Sami Burger, and found it hard to reconcile the freckle-faced girl with the beautiful woman sitting across from him, eating her pizza.

Stan caught him studying Sami, and shot him an even darker look.

Maybe if he spent time with the Williamses tomorrow, he'd be able to win Stan over....

Chapter Three

Normally, Sundays were quiet. Harry would get the newspaper from the front porch of his rental home and spend an hour or two lazing his way through it, a cup of coffee in hand. Then he'd either work on projects for the classes he was taking, or maybe deal with Erie Elementary business.

He made it a practice of doing something nonschool-related in the afternoon. Rollerblading around the paths along the peninsula, enjoying the increasingly colorful fall foliage, taking a long walk...something leisurely. He'd cap the day by treating himself to a home-cooked meal. Unfortunately, Harry's idea of a home-cooked meal meant a frozen dinner in the microwave.

That might explain why he'd awakened with a slightly embarrassing bubble of excitement that made his normal Sunday activities seem ponderous, rather than peaceful. He couldn't wait to go to the Williams house.

He kept assuring himself that it was the idea of real food that made the day seem so appealing, but he suspected the majority of his anticipation had nothing to do with meat loaf, and everything to do with Samantha Williams.

At ten to twelve, he drove to the address she'd given

him and realized he probably could have walked from his Grandview Boulevard town house.

Samantha's home was maybe a half mile away, on the north side of 38th Street. It was a two-story brick home with a large front porch that spanned the width of it. There was an unconnected garage in the back. Its door was open and it was crammed with bikes and skateboards, a huge soccer net…everything a houseful of kids could want.

He climbed the stairs, suddenly feeling a bit like an interloper. He'd practically invited himself. Samantha didn't need another mouth to feed. The bottle of wine in his hand felt like an inadequate hostess gift.

Before he could think of a way to apologize for the coerced invitation, the door opened.

"Hi, Harry." Samantha looked genuinely pleased to see him, and some of his trepidation dissolved.

He held the bottle of wine out to her. "I didn't know what else to bring. I was feeling bad because I sort of forced you to ask me."

Samantha laughed. Not some girly titter, but the full-bodied sound of a woman. "Harry, don't flatter yourself, no one forces me into anything. If I didn't genuinely want you here, I'd have ignored your not-so-subtle hints."

"But it did make extra work."

"It's just meat loaf and mashed potatoes. Nothing special. And cooking for six isn't any harder than cooking for five." She looked startled. "Where are my manners. Come in."

She stepped back and held the door open to him. Harry stepped into a crowded foyer. A coat tree was littered with various jackets and sweatshirts. Rollerblades, sneakers and a very pink pair of plastic slip-on shoes.

"Well, I'm glad you did pick up on my not-so-subtle

hints. After eating my own cooking, such as it is, since school started, meat loaf is very special."

"Mom made the pumpkin pies," Shane hollered as he poked his head around the corner.

"I can smell them." He turned to Samantha. "May I help?"

"No. I'm fine. Let me just finish it all off. You can make yourself at home in the living room. The kids will entertain you." She gestured through the doorway. The room said *lived in.* It was clean, and Harry could tell Samantha had straightened it for him, but there was no disguising the fact four kids called this place home. The slightly scuffed toe of a sneaker peeked out from under the couch. A video gaming system was plugged into the ports on the front of the TV, the cords snaking down to the machine. A stack of school books sat on the coffee table, and a *TV Guide* was folded to what Harry assumed was the appropriate day, with a remote control next to it.

The room said Family, with a capital *F.*

This was the sort of room a person looked forward to coming home to. The thought sent him a small stab of regret, which he immediately and purposefully squelched.

Three Williams kids—Shane, Seton and Stella— stood waiting for him.

Seton obviously couldn't wait any longer. "Come see our rooms, Mr. Rem."

"Sure. That sounds like fun." Harry started to follow the boy to the foyer and the stairs, when a low growling stopped him in his tracks.

"Grunge, cut that out," Stella scolded as she reached under the chair and pulled out a cat. At least, Harry assumed it was a cat. It was missing a patch of its ginger- colored hair at its left shoulder blade and one eye didn't seem to open. Yet it made up for the lack by glaring at Harry all the fiercer through its good eye.

"You scared the poor little kitty," Stella informed him.

"I scared *him?*" Harry asked. Poor little kitty indeed. The feral cat had a look about him that said he'd like to make Harry his dinner.

"Yeah, he gets scared by new people. His old people weren't so very nice to poor old Grunge." Stella stroked the hissing monstrosity's head.

"He just showed up at the back door one day," Shane informed him. "Mom started feeding him. It took two weeks before he'd let her hold him. For a long time he wouldn't stay in the house, but it got cold last winter and finally he did."

"Mom says that means he's a smart cat," Seton added. "He loves her and brings her presents all the time."

"Presents?" Harry asked, wondering if it was wise.

"Mice, toads and once a snake." Shane reached over and patted the savage cat's head.

"He never kills them," Seton assured Harry.

"He's a guard cat." Stella squeezed the cat tighter.

Harry half expected the cat to turn and bite her. Instead, he could swear Grunge sighed as he cast Harry a look that said he was used to being mauled by the eight-year-old, but that he'd survive.

"Once Bobby followed me home and was yelling, but Grunge came out and chased him away. I told everyone at school Bobby was a scaredy cat. I mean, scared of a cat." She laughed while her brothers both groaned.

"That's still not funny, Stell," Seton assured her. "Right, Mr. Rem?"

"I liked it, Stella." Sensing an argument in the making, he chose to divert the kids' attention away from the cat. "Now, you were going to show me your rooms?"

They led him up the stairs and eagerly showed off the biggest room, which was where all three boys slept. Stan was sitting on the single bed, and didn't offer a greeting. He just flipped over and turned his back to Harry. Shane and Seton showed him their bunk beds and various treasures that ranged from rocks to rockets.

Stella led him across the hall to a terminally pink room. It was tiny, but it seemed to suit the youngster and her dolls. And there were enough dolls to have given his boyhood self nightmares. But now, in his mid-thirties, he was man enough to confess there was something endearing about not just the room, but in Stella introducing him to all her dolls, one by one.

The two boys stood in the doorway groaning, but Stella continued with the introductions until she got to the very last doll, who was obviously special, sitting dead center of Stella's bed. "And this is Miss Ruby, Mr. Rem." She used the boys' abbreviated version of his name. "She's going to come have dinner with us, aren't you, Miss Ruby?"

Ruby must have responded in the positive because Stella scooped her up and said, "Come on, Mr. Rem. We all have to wash our hands, or mom won't let us eat."

"Stell—" Shane started to say.

Stella obviously knew what was coming because she interrupted him. "And, yes, I will tell if you don't."

"She thinks she's thirty," Seton stage-whispered to Harry.

"Or our mom," Shane added. "And that's not such a good thing, 'cause we've already got one too many."

"You can't have enough people to care about you. Little sisters included."

Stella turned around and stuck her tongue out at her

brothers, and Harry stifled a grin. "Enough of that, Stella," he said in his best principal voice.

They all trooped into the bathroom and washed their hands in turn under Stella's watchful eyes.

As they walked back to the stairs, Harry caught a glimpse of Samantha's bedroom through the crack in the door. It was all earth tones and pillows, the combination of which said comfort. It did something funny to his stomach, making it give a quick flip.

He was glad to get back downstairs where it smelled of pumpkin pies and meat loaf.

"Dinner," Samantha announced, right on cue.

"My hands are washed, Mommy," Stella called out. "I made sure they all washed, too, except for Stan. He was pouting."

"I wasn't pouting," Stan informed his sister as he came into the room, his expression dark and stormy. "And I don't need an eight-year-old telling me to wash for dinner."

"You do, too." Stella turned to Harry. "None of the boys like washin' their hands, but me and Miss Ruby don't mind, do we, Miss Ruby?" She paused as if listening to the doll. "Yeah, right. Boys are gross."

"Mom, Stella's got that doll at the table again," Shane pointed out. "She's not allowed to, Mr. Rem. Mom says if Ruby needs to be fed, she has to wait until Stella's had her whole meal first. Stella always remembers about handwashing, but never remembers the no-doll-at-the-table rule."

"It's a stupid rule," Stella grumbled as she got up and carefully deposited Ruby on the windowsill before coming back to the table.

"Is not," Seton assured his sister. "Not after you set the table on fire because of Ruby."

"Table on fire?" Harry tried to imagine how a doll could ignite a table, but was at a loss.

"I didn't do it, Seton did. Miss Ruby was just sittin' on the table next to my plate, and he reached across to steal her, and when I grabbed her, we hit the candle."

"It fell," Seton picked up the tale and continued, "And landed on a stack of paper napkins. There's still a mark on the table under the tablecloth." He sounded almost proud.

"And on Miss Ruby. She got burned all over her tummy. So Daddy—" Stella started, then abruptly stopped.

"So after that," Samantha seamlessly explained as she set a platter of meat loaf slices in the center of the table, "Ruby was relegated to the windowsill during dinner, and Seton had to help his sister clean her room for a whole week."

"'Cause Ruby had to be in the hospital to get better, and I couldn't clean my room and take care of her, right, Mom?"

"Right," Samantha agreed.

"But Ruby still can't come to the table." Stella cast a wistful look at her doll.

"And right now, we have dinner, so let's all pretend this isn't the type of family who sets tables and dolls on fire and impress Mr. Remington with our manners. Okay?"

The meal was a cacophony of noise. Grace was said, serving platters and bowls were passed. The kids all ate with gusto and finished long before Harry had even made a dent in his meat loaf.

"Can I be excused?" Stan, the only quiet child at the table, asked.

Samantha looked concerned, but nodded. "Yes, you may."

He stomped away.

"Us, too?" the other three children asked in unison.

"Sure. But you're on cleanup duty. I'll call when I'm ready for you." Grumbling among themselves about the unfairness of cleanup duty, the kids tromped out of the room.

The dining room was plunged into silence, which seemed out of place after all that noise.

Samantha sighed. "Listen to that… I know my kids don't really eat as much as inhale their meals, and that if I were a really good mother, I would insist they eat slower, like civilized people. But, between you and me, Harry, very selfishly, I don't. I very much enjoy the short quiet respite after they've finished to do anything that might delay it."

He laughed. "That's devious, Sami."

"It's called self-preservation. Would you like more wine?" Without waiting for an answer, she poured some into his glass, then her own. "This is delicious."

"I spent last Saturday touring the wineries in North East." A small town just outside of Erie, North East had a number of small, family-run wineries. Most people didn't think of Pennsylvania in connection with grapes and wine, but it was one of the larger grape-growing regions in the country. Welch's had a plant there and made jams and juices. "It's a beautiful place. I'll confess, I bought a number of bottles."

"Well, I'm glad you shared." She took another sip. "Can I get you anything else?"

"No. I'm fine. Everything's perfect. I can't tell you when I had a meal this good."

She looked flustered by the compliment. "Thanks, but it's not anything fancy." She paused, then said, "We seem to have a few extra quiet minutes. Tell me about your life after you moved to Ohio."

"Let's see, how to sum up the last twenty years? Mom and I moved to Columbus. I started at a new school. A year later, she remarried. My mom and step-father had two more kids. Dad remarried, as well, and they had three more kids."

"Who did you live with?"

"I sort of felt like an outcast in both families, so I stayed with my grandparents." He couldn't believe he'd just confessed that. Feeling awkward, he hurried on, hoping Samantha wouldn't comment. "I didn't want to change schools again. So, I finished high school there, then went to OSU."

He expected her to push, to tell him that of course both his parents loved him and would have welcomed him into their homes. He'd heard it before from his grandparents and parents. It might have been true, but that didn't alter the fact that he felt out of place in each of his parents' new lives.

But Samantha didn't push. Instead, she asked, "You planned to be a principal?"

"No. Actually, I have a degree in journalism. I worked for a few papers, but discovered I wanted something more. I couldn't figure out what until we had a school tour come through the paper. We had a staff lottery, and I lost."

"Lost?" She took a sip of the wine.

"Loser led the tour," he admitted ruefully. "But really, I won. Talking to the kids, seeing them light up and get enthusiastic…" He shrugged. "I just knew I'd figured it out. I got emergency certification, but went back to school nights and got a degree in education. I moved into administration last year as an assistant principal. I'm taking classes at Edinboro in order to finish my administration degree."

"So, what brought you back to Erie, just school?"

His one small slip of utter truthfulness was all he could manage to indulge in. He didn't lie, but he didn't need to give Samantha full disclosure, either. "I needed a change of scenery. I didn't plan on working, but Geri asked if I'd help her out and fill in at Erie Elementary until she found a new principal."

"And here you are. Back where you started." She smiled as if that was a good thing.

"Yes. Back where I started."

"Did you ever marry?"

Harry knew that Samantha had no way of knowing her question was like rubbing salt in an open wound. And he didn't go into details as he simply shook his head. "Came close, but no, I never married."

Again, she didn't push. She just reached across the table and covered his hand with hers. "I'm sorry."

"Your turn."

"I married, had four kids, and divorced. That's it in a nutshell. Not overly exciting, but I'm happy."

"I'm sorry about the divorce."

"I am, too. Not so much for me. I'm surprisingly all right." She wore a puzzled look, as if she wasn't quite sure how it was that she was all right. "We were so young when we married. I was still in college. I think the marriage ended a long time before either of us admitted it. It hurt, but I think it was for the best…for us at least. Not the kids. Watching them go through it hurt me more than the divorce itself. The fact their father ignores them hurts them all. I can see it, and it's frustrating not being able to do anything about it. And you've looked at the boys' files. I don't know what else to do for them."

He realized her hand was still on top of his, so he

flipped his and they were palm to palm. He gave her hand a squeeze.

"Wow, that was far more serious than I'd intended. What do you say we forget about the past, and look to the future? I predict it will be sweet." She raised her wineglass.

Harry raised his own glass and toasted with her. "To a sweet future for both of us." They each took a sip. "So do you often predict the future?"

"In this case, it wasn't hard. I know of a certain pumpkin pie cooling on the counter. I guarantee it's sweet." She grinned.

"Maybe we could go out sometime," he found himself blurting out.

"Pardon?"

"You and me. Out. Dinner or something."

"Harry, I don't—"

"Just two old friends having some fun."

"Oh, of course, that makes sense. You know, after Phillip left me, I lost my old circle of friends. I don't know if they backed away from me or if I backed away from them, but regardless, I've been lonely. I didn't even notice it until I got stuck on the Social Planning Committee with Michelle and Carly, but looking back, I see how lonely I've been this last year. And I know I don't want to be that way again, so yes, going out with a friend for dinner or something some night would be very nice."

"I don't know anyone here in town, so I'd welcome a friend, as well." Harry needed to be sure she understood it couldn't be more than friendship. He'd sworn that he'd never date a woman with a child again. And Samantha had four. As much as he enjoyed the Williams family, he'd never allow it to go any further than friendship.

"Then you've got a date, at least in a two-friends-having-dinner-but-not-really-dating sort of way. I don't know—"

Whatever it was Samantha didn't know, Harry would also never know, because at that moment a hellacious noise came from the living room.

"Sorry," she blurted, even as she jumped out of her chair and raced toward the door. "We'll have to finish this later."

She disappeared from sight, and Harry could hear her refereeing. "Boys, you know better than picking up Grunge."

"But, Mom—"

"No, buts…"

Harry smiled as he listened. Samantha was firm, but loving. She'd seemed so surprised when he suggested they go out.

To be honest, so was he.

Because despite telling Samantha he just needed a buddy, there was something more. An attraction there that wasn't quite a platonic friendship. As a matter of fact, when she was toasting their sweet future, he'd been thinking how sweet it would be to kiss her, and that thought alone was a shock.

Oh, he'd noted that she was a good-looking woman. There was no denying that. However, he'd met a lot of good-looking women since Teresa had left him, and none of them had made him think about kissing them to the degree that Samantha Williams had.

"Now, go find Stella and tell her to bring Grunge down. We'll all have pumpkin pie before Mr. Remington has to leave. Then all you guys have to tackle the cleanup."

He heard footsteps on the stairs, and Samantha reentered the room. "Sorry about that. Chaos rules this house. At least it does when the kids are around."

"I deal with kids every day. I'm immune to chaos."

SAMANTHA WASN'T SURE that dealing with kids at school could really equal dealing with them at home, but she let Harry have his illusion.

Stella ran into the room, Ruby in one hand, Grunge in the other. "Grunge and me are ready for pie."

"Stella, we've had this discussion before," Samantha reminded her daughter. "Cats don't eat people food."

"But most cats eat mice, and Grunge never does. So, maybe since he doesn't like cat food, he'd like people food better."

"There's a certain logic to your argument," Samantha agreed with a smile, "but still we're not giving the cat people food. It could make him sick."

"Mice could make him sick. They've got bones and stuff. Pumpkin pie never would. It doesn't even have any seeds in it."

"Stella, put the cat and doll down, if you want a piece yourself…."

"No Ruby, Stella. No Grunge, Stella," the little girl mimicked as she put the cat on the floor and her doll on the windowsill. "I don't get nothin', Mom."

"You get pie. And a family who loves you. That's a lot."

Stella didn't look convinced as she took her seat.

Stan entered the room, still glowering, although Samantha didn't have any idea about what. Stan was thirteen, and she was discovering that thirteen-year-olds didn't need any real reason to sulk. The expression seemed to come naturally with the teenage territory.

And Harry was still sitting in his seat, watching them all. She wondered if he was regretting his impromptu invitation. And she knew he hadn't planned on suggesting they have dinner by the surprised look on his face as he'd said the words.

She was equally confused by the fact she'd said yes. Chapter Two in *How to Be Happy Without Really Trying* suggested that in order to be happy you had to accept you had a right to be happy. And she'd known as he'd asked, going out to dinner with Harry would make her happy. It wasn't a date, and that was actually comforting. She wasn't sure if she was ready to date.

She dished up the slices of pie and took them into the dining room. "Okay, everyone dig in." Her fork made it halfway to her mouth before the doorbell rang.

She wasn't sure who to expect on a Sunday, but when she opened the door and found her ex-husband there, it wasn't even on her list of possibilities.

"Phillip?"

"Sorry to just drop in, but I was hoping you had some time. I want to make arrangements to have the kids over more regularly, now that I'm settled."

"You do?"

"Don't look so surprised, Sam."

She tried to school her expression, but clearly she wasn't doing a very good job of it. "Sorry. It's just, it's been a year—"

"I know. I was in a bad place for a very long time, but I'm better now, and Lois says—" He cut himself off.

"I know about Lois. It's okay, Phillip," she told him gently. And it was. "I'm happy if you've found someone who makes you happy."

He didn't look as if he quite believed her. "So, can I come in?"

Samantha nodded. "Sure. We were just finishing up dinner."

"I don't want to interrupt."

"You're not." Well, he was. Though Samantha wasn't about to tell him that. Not after wanting so desperately for him to spend time with the kids.

As they walked into the dining room, the kids cried, "Dad." She saw Harry's look of surprise, and turned to find Phillip staring as if he'd been caught off guard, as well.

She felt guilty.

She knew she had no reason to. She was divorced, and Phillip had someone living with him, for Pete's sake. She had every right to invite Harry to dinner.

Still, there it was—guilt.

She knew she needed to say something to smooth this over. Harry stood, and walked around the table. "Harry. Harry Remington."

"Phillip Williams."

They shook, and Samantha felt even more awkward than before. "Sorry. Phil, Harry's the kids' principal. He treated us to pizza yesterday, so we're treating him to pumpkin pie today."

"I see." Phillip cast her a speculative look. "Maybe we should do this some other time?"

"No, that's not necessary," Harry said almost too quickly. "You two do whatever it is you need to do. I've finished my pie—and Sami, it was just as delicious as the kids said. I'll see myself out."

"Let me walk you to the door." When they reached the semi-quiet foyer, she said, "I'm sorry about the inter-ruption. I'd have asked him to do it later, it's just—"

"He's showing an interest and you want to encourage it. I get that. It's all right. But if he's going to take the kids for a night, do you think we could have that date?"

"A date, you say?" The word made her nervous, so

she clarified, "Sure. A dinner between two old friends. I'd like that."

"I look forward to it." He glanced behind her. "Talk to you soon to set a date."

There it was, that word again.

Samantha stood at the door and watched him leave, feeling bemused. She had a date.

The realization sank in.

He'd originally asked her to go out to dinner, no mention of the word date.

But he'd said the word *date*.

Twice.

So were they going out to dinner, a couple of old friends? Or was it a *date?*

She didn't know, and she was rather afraid to find out.

Chapter Four

"Help," Samantha said as an opening greeting that Friday at the next meeting of the PTA moms.

Michelle and Carly were both already at the Erie Elementary meeting room when she arrived.

"Hi, Samantha," Carly said. "What do you need help with?"

"The Thanksgiving Pageant?" Michelle asked.

Samantha sank into a vacant chair. "No, not the pageant. Worse. You see, I'm confused. I agreed to go out to dinner with an old friend. An old *male* friend."

Okay, so maybe *old friend* was a generous description. When she was in fifth grade, it was unthinkable being the friend of a seventh-grade boy. The two groups traveled in separate stratospheres. "Maybe an old acquaintance is a better description. The point is, I agreed to just a dinner, but he used the word *date*. Twice. Once he said, you've got a date, and the second time he just talked about setting a date, so maybe that was just picking a day. Hmm, maybe I'm only worried about him using the word once. Or maybe I'm nervous about having dinner with a man, even in the most platonic sense."

Samantha felt better simply taking about her concern.

"I could really use some advice…well, after we do the business part of tonight's meeting."

"Business can wait," Carly assured her. "I brought éclairs from Traditions." She opened the box. "And three coffees. We'll talk as we have our snack, *then* we'll get to our business."

Samantha eyed the hoagie-sized confections and she sucked her stomach in tight. The éclair, on top of Sunday's pumpkin pie and its leftovers, meant she'd be sucking in her stomach through the holiday if she indulged. "Those can't be éclairs…I mean, they're huge."

"They don't mess around at that bakery. I love going to the market. Urbaniak's has the best meat department." Carly chose one of the sweet confections, placed it on a napkin and pulled it toward her. "Come on, help yourselves. I even brought forks."

Accept happiness, she reminded herself. Chapter Two of *How to Be Happy Without Really Trying* was quite explicit. And she knew she'd be happier with an éclair than without. So she took hers and allowed herself to savor the first bite.

Éclairs and coffee distributed, Michelle said, "Now, spill. Who's the date—that maybe's not a date—with, and where's he taking you?"

"No, I've decided I just panicked. It's not a date. We'd clarified that it wasn't a date, so it isn't."

"Come on, drama queen. No need to drag it out." Carly laughed. "Who is it?"

Samantha didn't see any point in beating around the bush, so she blurted out, "Harry Remington."

"Who?" Carly asked.

"Mr. Remington, the new principal. His first name is Harry, Heidi said," Michelle reminded Carly.

They both eyed Samantha curiously.

She swallowed the éclair and nodded. "Yes, the principal."

"Oh. So, I guess that meeting with him went well?" Carly laughed again and took a disgustingly huge bite of her éclair.

"It did. You see…" She filled them in on everything from her first meeting with Harry, recalling how she'd known him when they were younger, to the boys' detention and subsequent pizza outing, to Sunday dinner. "So we were going to go out sometime for dinner, and then he called it a date."

"Hold on," Carly said around a huge bite of éclair. "Is it a date, or a dinner thing, like you might go on with me and Michelle?"

"That's just it, I don't know."

"Which do you want it to be?" Michelle asked quietly.

Now, that was the other question she'd been wrangling with.

"I don't know that, either, and I don't know why I don't know. Harry's cute and sweet. I should be hoping it's a date-date, but I'm not. I'm dreading that it is. He's an interim principal—only in Erie for a short time. Even if it was a date-date, it couldn't go anywhere. And there's not much I'm certain about, except the fact that I'm not ready to date. Balancing the kids, work and now the Thanksgiving Pageant is all I can manage. I don't think I could juggle dating. A dinner with a friend, yes, but not dating."

That was the truth, but not all of it. Things might have been stagnant between her and Phillip for a long time, but when he'd told her he was leaving, she'd been blindsided. She'd hurt so much. All she'd wanted to do was crawl into a hole and stay there. But she couldn't. The kids had been hurt and confused. She'd had to get up and keep going for their sakes. And slowly, each day, her own pain seemed to have ebbed. Eventually, she could think of Phillip without it hurting. She could remember the good times, and there had been good times.

Now, more than a year removed from him walking out, she felt as if she'd healed. Although that didn't mean she was ready to go through that kind of pain again. And dating meant considering a relationship. She wasn't ready for that risk.

"Maybe that's the way to get back into dating, with a rebound man, a relationship that can't go anywhere," Carly said.

"Actually, there might be something nice about a relationship with no strings, no expectations." Michelle sounded wistful.

Carly looked intrigued with the idea. "When I get back into the dating circuit—if I get back into the dating circuit—it will be casual all the way. I'd want a quiet man. Someone who wouldn't tell me what I should do, and shouldn't do. Someone who won't mind me standing on my own two feet because I guarantee you that I won't ever count on someone else again. Been there, done that and discovered I didn't really enjoy the experience."

"I don't think it's a date-date," Samantha said with a little more confidence. "He had a bad break in his past." She thought about the flash of pain on his face when she'd asked if he'd ever married. She'd felt both pity and a bond of kinship with him at that moment. "So, I don't think it is."

"If it is, it's casual. Like you said, he's leaving in December, it can't be anything but casual, so why stress about it?" Carly asked.

"I don't know how to casually date a man," Samantha

admitted. "I mean, the last man I dated was Phillip, and we ended up married for fourteen years. Harry would be temporary to the nth degree. I don't know how to manage that."

"Is it really managing something? An old friend who will take you out on the town," Carly asked.

"Samantha," Michelle finally said, "Brandon came to live with me right after I got out of college, and I'll confess he's my focus. So my dates are few and far between. But Carly's right. This sounds perfect. It doesn't matter if it's a real date or just a dinner. You're two old friends. You don't have to call him, he doesn't have to call you, afterward. There are no expectations, beyond this one dinner. And if you go out after that, then you know there's an expiration date in the not-so-distant future."

"But like I said, I've never casually dated before. I mean, how many dates can you go on without…well, I mean, I'm not sure I'm ready to be intimate with a man I'm not serious about."

"And nothing says you have to be," Michelle said gently. "You can date someone without having sex."

"You can?" Carly gave a cynical little laugh, then sighed. "That was my attempt to sound worldly. When in actuality, I've been out of the dating pool so long, I'm not quite ready to even try dunking my toes in, much less diving into the deep end."

"So, if you find out it is a date, tell Harry that you'd be happy to dunk your toes with him, but you're not ready for the deep end, either," Michelle counseled.

"Do you think he'll be okay with that?" She felt like one of her kids, asking questions, needing reassurance.

"I think that if he's not, he's not the kind of man you want to date." Michelle seemed so much older than Samantha knew she was.

"So when is this dinner?"

"Tomorrow." Her stomach did a little flutter at the thought. "Phillip's taking the kids for the whole weekend. He picked them up today after school, and I don't get them again until Sunday. He's taking them again next weekend, then planning to try every other weekend after that. I'm just so happy he's taking an interest in them again."

"He didn't take them for a year. He can afford to be accommodating now," Carly said. "So are you splitting the holidays? It took a long time for my ex and I to figure out how to manage that. We didn't part on good terms."

"We've both really worked at being civil. I guess that's the word to describe the end of our marriage and our divorce—civil."

And since Samantha loved the kids, *civil* wasn't hard while sorting out Phillip's visitation. "The holidays weren't difficult to arrange. Halloween will fall on Phillip's weekend, so he'll take them trick-or-treating on Friday, then bring them home Saturday so that I can take them to the school's party. I'll get them Thanksgiving Day. He'll pick them up that evening and keep them through the break. Christmas we'll divide the same way."

"It sounds amicable," Carly said.

Amicable, just another word for *civil.*

Both were synonymous with passionless. Was that lack of passion why their marriage faltered? Maybe it was why their divorce was going so well?

"You're a good mother," Michelle said. "I don't think it goes that smoothly with all divorced parents."

"Anyway," Carly said, "we're not worrying about my lousy ex, but your upcoming date."

Samantha's stomach did another flip at the thought. "Don't call it that."

"Dinner," Carly substituted.

"I'm so afraid I'll screw up. I mean, do I tell him up front I'm not looking for an intimate relationship? How many dates can a woman go on without putting out? Do they even say *putting out* anymore? I'm thirty-three. I expected to feel more worldly, but the truth of it is, I feel as uncertain as when I was in my teens. When I agreed to dinner with Harry, even though I knew he was leaving, did he think I was agreeing to…"

"Put out?" Carly added with a grin.

Samantha laughed, despite her nerves. "Yes."

"My advice?" Michelle said in her quiet, unflappable way. "Take a deep breath. You don't have to decide anything now. If he's the kind of man you want to date, he'll cut you some slack and understand that you're taking it slow. And if he doesn't understand, dump him."

Michelle's words settled something in Samantha. "You're right."

"Dating is a time to get to know someone," Michelle continued. "To have fun. And seriously, listening to you and Carly dealing with kids and exes, I think you're both due a bit of fun."

"Not me," Carly proclaimed adamantly. "I'm done with that kind of fun. I'm going to concentrate on my kids, work and finishing my degree. I don't have time for men."

"What about fun for you?" Samantha asked Michelle. She was the youngest of them. Michelle should be out partying with friends and having the time of her life. Instead, she talked of taxes and her nephew. "You need to have fun, too."

"My sister was the fun one. I was always the serious

bookworm. And I guess that's how I'm most comfortable. Now—" she wore an expression that said the part of the conversation where she was in the spotlight was over "—it's time for a *serious* conversation…anyone want to split another éclair?"

All three women laughed, and they finally stopped talking about Samantha's date, and focused on the Thanksgiving Pageant. "I think Mrs. Tarbot and I have it all under control. She's scheduled it for the twenty-fifth. That's our last day of school before Thanksgiving vacation starts. They're doing a play this year. There's not much for you two to worry about. The fourth grade is singing a song before the play, and the second- and first-graders are singing one at the end of it. The big part is the third-grade play. If you wouldn't mind helping backstage at the actual pageant, the rest should be fine."

"Great. I've started classes. Only two more credits left before I get my nursing degree. It's been a long time coming," Carly said.

Samantha spoke up, "And I meant to tell you, Dr. Jackson said you're welcome to come into his pediatric office one day and shadow me. Interning at St. Vincent's Hospital is one thing, but it's a whole different feel at a private practice."

Samantha liked working in a private practice so much better than a hospital and wanted to be sure Carly got a taste of the difference.

"I'd love to shadow you, tell him thanks. And I'm so glad you have most of the pageant under control. Between the kids, the classes and the hospital, I'm crazy busy. I keep telling myself that I'll have my degree in December and that all this will be worth it then."

"Don't wish away my fall," Michelle warned. "Accountants love fall because we know that when winter starts it's almost tax season." She groaned for effect.

Samantha and Carly both laughed.

"Oh, one more thing," Michelle added. "Heidi asked if we'd be willing to help her with the school's Halloween party. Halloween's on a Friday, so they're doing a Saturday afternoon thing. We don't have to plan, or do anything, other than show up at school that day and follow orders."

Samantha was pretty sure that was her Saturday morning off, and if it wasn't she could wiggle out of work for the day. Dr. Jackson was a firm believer in family first, and tried to accommodate everyone on the staff. "Sure, I'm in."

Carly and Michelle agreed, as well. Business done, they all started talking about their kids. The three had no trouble keeping that particular conversation going for an extended period of time. Any mother—or aunt, in Michelle's case—usually could. So, it was an hour later when Samantha left. She purposefully sucked in her stomach to hopefully compensate for the éclairs. She felt better, and it had nothing to do with her sugar high.

No, it had everything to do with discovering two new friends.

Accept your right to be happy, the book had said.

Phillip stepping back into the kids' lives made her happy.

Two new friends made her happy.

Dinner with Harry? That made her nervous, but underneath that, she was pretty sure it made her happy, as well.

Maybe she was ready to start Chapter Three?

THE ENTIRE WEEK PASSED at a snail's pace for Harry.

He'd been looking forward to Saturday, but now that it was here he was nervous.

He kept reminding himself that he was a grown man. That this was merely dinner with an old friend.

It didn't help.

He surreptitiously glanced at his watch, hoping his classmates didn't notice. One of his reasons for taking a sabbatical was to finish the last classes he needed for his Education Administration degree. This was why he'd come back to Western PA. Edinboro had a great program. Though try as he might, he couldn't concentrate on the class. Images of Samantha kept getting in the way.

Mingling with the nervousness over tonight's dinner was a sense of anticipation.

It was just a dinner. But it didn't feel like that. It felt like a date. And dating Samantha would be a mistake. They were both getting over failed relationships, and he'd be going back to Columbus, while Samantha would be staying here.

And Samantha was a mother of four.

Harry had vowed to never let himself fall for another woman who had kids. Not because he didn't like kids, but because if a relationship failed, you didn't lose just the woman, but you also lost a child you'd given your heart to.

With Samantha, he risked losing his heart five times over. As much as he liked her, he wasn't willing to go through that again for anyone.

No, dating Samantha Williams was out of the question.

This was dinner, he assured himself.

Unfortunately, he didn't believe it.

He glanced at his watch again. Twenty-five minutes till class got out.

Little Sami Burger.

She'd been two years younger than him, and cute in a puppy dog sort of way. He hadn't shared that analogy with her because he was pretty sure she wouldn't find it flattering, but it was the truth.

She'd had a spattering of freckles across the bridge of her nose. She'd worn glasses and pigtails. And she was forever bumping into things.

There was no puppy dog cuteness about her anymore. She'd been doggedly protective when she'd come to his office that first day, the expression she'd worn had said that she was willing to take on anyone who messed with her kids. She'd battled Tooly the year before, and had been willing to battle the new principal for her boys' sakes.

He found that fierceness so very attractive.

Harry glanced at the clock on the far wall. Twenty minutes to go.

Even when he was twelve, Sami Burger had been hard to figure out. He didn't expect Samantha Williams to be any easier. He hadn't been sure she'd say yes to dinner. She'd been ready to say no, he thought. But something had changed her mind. And he was glad of it, because he liked her a lot.

He liked her kids.

He liked her concern for her kids.

Liked the fact she was willing to work with her ex for the kids' benefit.

He liked her pumpkin pie.

He even kind of liked her one-eyed cat. Well, as long as he didn't have to pick the thing up, he kind of liked it.

All of which made him nervous about tonight's da— Dinner.

He glanced at his watch. Fifteen minutes to go.

SAMANTHA GLANCED AT THE mirror next to the front door. She fluffed her hair, and didn't think the new cut was half-bad. She'd gone to the salon as soon as she'd finished work at Dr. Jackson's. She'd planned on having a trim, but she found herself asking for a whole new look.

Rachel had practically cackled with glee as she juggled two other appointments so she could spend the next two hours working on Samantha's do.

Samantha had endured the foils, the smell of the bleach and heat lamps, all of which had given her the most subtle highlights. If that wasn't enough, she then had to sit for the cut, and at Rachel's insistence, she'd even endured a manicure.

Now, looking in the foyer's mirror, she sucked in her stomach and realized this was as good as she got. And she looked pretty good.

She wouldn't worry about whether or not this was a date. She wasn't going to worry that she hadn't been out to dinner with any man other than Phillip in over a decade. She was simply going to enjoy herself.

The doorbell rang. She jumped and she adjusted an imaginary wrinkle on her sleeve to stall for a moment before she opened the door. "Hi, Harry."

"Hi, Samantha." He paused, then said, "Wow."

It was exactly what she needed to hear. Some of her nervousness eased and she finally relaxed. "Come in. I just need to grab a jacket."

He stepped into the foyer and she reached into the coat closet.

"The house feels different without the kids in it."

Samantha paused. The only sound was Grunge, doing his patrol-cat growl because Harry had entered the premises. "It does. Before Phillip started taking the kids, I never had to deal with it. Now that I do I'm not quite sure how to manage it. The first night was nice, a treat. But I'm not sure it will always feel like a treat. I don't know what to do with myself."

She'd been the one to push for Phillip to spend time with the kids, and she was genuinely glad that he was, but she missed them. Missed the chaos and noise.

She understood what Harry meant. "Sorry. Not the best way to start a d—" Date? Dinner?

Harry paused, as if waiting for her to define what tonight was.

"Dinner with an old friend," she said, settling for the description she had used with Carly and Michelle.

He looked disappointed, but then he laughed and said, "Hey, we're not that old yet."

Samantha decided she must have imagined the negative expression. "You're right, we're not."

Before Samantha could swing her jacket on, Harry took it. "Let me help you."

Part of her wanted to protest that she was capable of putting her own coat on, that, in fact, she'd spent the last year taking care of herself and her kids. But the other part that had spent the last year taking care of herself and her kids relished the small gesture of someone taking care of her. She felt cherished.

She allowed herself that moment as Harry slipped her sleeves up over her bare arms and pulled the collar up against her neck. She felt a wisp of air against her neck's exposed skin and wondered if it was from the motion of pulling the coat on, or if it was Harry's breath, offering her a small caress.

"Uh, thank you."

As if he'd read her mind, he said, "I know you could have done it yourself, but every now and again a man likes to play the gallant. Seriously, look at it from a guy's point of view, it's hard to know what to do. Open the door for a lady, or let her open it herself? Hold a chair for her, or not? I tend to err on the side of gallantry."

That said, he gave a bow, opened the door with as much flourish as she'd ever seen, and waited for her to go through.

She laughed, a bit more of her tension easing off.

Harry was really getting into the courtly swing of things, and continued his chivalrous treatment as he opened her car door and gently shut it behind her, before getting into the car himself.

"So, where are we going?" she asked.

"I was talking to a friend and he had a suggestion…" He paused. "It sounded good at the time, but it seems a bit…well, over-the-top now. I wanted to impress you and he insisted the La Bonne Vie Steakhouse was the way to impress a first date."

"Harry, you don't have to impress me. I'd have been happy with fast food, as long as I got some adult conversation."

"See, that's what I was afraid of. It was overkill. So when we get there, pretend it's not, okay?"

"Okay."

Harry had been as anxious and confused as she'd been, Samantha realized.

He'd said he'd almost married and she wondered how long ago the *almost* was? She wanted to ask, but it seemed too abrupt, so she didn't. She just sat back and enjoyed the ride as they drove towards I-90.

There was something so lovely about this time of day. Not quite night, the dusk growing heavier by the minute. They drove up Old French Street. She and Harry didn't talk, but it wasn't one of those awkward silences. It was comfortable.

The sky was darkening as the sun brushed the western treetops, sinking behind them. "I love this time of day, when it's somewhere between daylight and night," Samantha murmured.

"It's a bit too ambiguous for my taste," Harry muttered. "I like things more straightforward than that."

"Are we still talking about dusk, or something else?" She cracked the car window, allowing the cool evening air to flood the car.

Harry glanced over at her, before looking back at the road. "Listen, Sam, I haven't done this in a long time."

"This?"

"Dinner with a woman. Well, not with a woman I wasn't committed to."

He was leaving her an opening to ask, so she obliged. "You said you'd almost married, and I'd wondered, was the breakup recent?"

He nodded. "We were together for seven years."

"Oh."

He'd said something before about a relationship that had ended. As he told her again, she could see the pain in his expression.

He shrugged, maybe trying to look nonchalant, but it didn't work. Samantha could see the hurt. "I'm sorry."

"I am, too. You asked why I took the sabbatical and I said to finish my graduate classes. That was the truth, as far as it went. More than that, I took it because I needed to get away from all the concerned looks and hushed questions. And though friends have called, it's somehow easier to handle their sympathy long-distance."

"I've noticed that. I'd like to hear what happened, if you'd like to tell me."

"I'd wanted to marry Teresa for a long time. She'd married young, had a son..." he hesitated, then continued. "She went through a rocky divorce. Teresa said she'd never go down that path again. I could either deal with that, or walk. So, we lived together. A family in every way, except a marriage certificate. I dealt with it because I loved her. Her son was like my son. Lucas was three when Teresa and I got together. He's ten now. I missed being with him on his birthday. I took him to his practices, watched him when she worked weekends. I was the one who held his hand when they put a cast on his leg. It's not fair. I lost her, and I lost him. When she turned down my proposal last spring, she dumped me and moved with her son Lucas back to her hometown."

He stopped the car for a red traffic light.

"Where do they live?" she asked.

"Topeka. So it's not like I can pop over and take him out for a game. I had a family, but she left and there was nothing I could do."

"Oh, Harry, I'm so sorry." She reached across the car and took his hand.

"This wasn't the conversation I had in mind for tonight. It's especially not the conversation I thought we would have before we even got to the restaurant."

"Harry, maybe it's easier because we're not really out in public. We're just two people talking in a car. I'm pretty sure that we could both come up with some superficial discussion. But you just shared something with me, something close and personal that allowed me to know you a bit better. That's a much better conversation, no matter how you cut it."

"Thanks. It's kind of you to say."

"Listen, I know you planned on a fancy meal, but since the two-people-talking-in-a-car thing is working so well for us, I almost hate to go somewhere. There's a McDonald's up ahead. We could go through the drive-thru and stay in the car and keep talking."

"Are you sure?"

"Positive."

They both got their Big Macs, fries and shakes, then Harry parked the car in a dark corner of the parking lot.

"This is perfect." Samantha ate a fry. "I mean, I can't tell you the last time I ate dinner in total quiet. Four kids and quiet don't tend to go hand-in-hand."

"This isn't quite the dinner I'd envisioned taking you on, but you're right, it's nice."

They ate in silence for a few minutes, then Samantha asked softly, "So, have you had any contact with Lucas?"

"Yeah. We e-mail back and forth, and talk on the phone a few times a week. I made sure it was okay with Teresa," he hastened to add.

"I never thought you didn't." She couldn't imagine losing both Phillip and her kids.

"It's not the same, though. Phone calls and e-mail can't take the place of being there with him, taking part in the mundane things. In and of themselves, they don't seem like much, but when you lose them, they're everything."

"You're right, it's not the same. I've never been able to understand how Phillip could have been so willing to let weeks and months go by without seeing or calling the kids."

"It sounds like that's changing now."

"It is. We talked and he admitted he's been in therapy for the last six months. He's feeling better, and he's starting a new life with Lois. I'm glad for him. But more than that, I'm glad for the kids."

"Well, we've officially covered our exes. Now what?"

"Isn't it a beautiful autumn night? That's a normal first-date topic," Samantha teased.

Harry laughed, and she did, as well. That bubble of

nervousness finally just popped and completely disappeared. This was Harry, and there was no pressure.

They talked about her kids, about Lucas, about the school. She made a small foray into politics, and though they didn't totally mesh, they debated their differences comfortably, neither trying to convert the other.

They talked themselves through the Big Macs and fries, and walked inside to the counter for sundaes for dessert

Samantha was pretty sure this had to be the best first date in the history of dates, if it was a first date.

Two hours later, when Harry saw her home, he walked her to the front door. "Thanks, Sami." He grinned as he used her old nickname.

"This was a wonderful night, Harry." She didn't ask if it was a date, because it didn't matter. She didn't need to define the night with Harry. It was what it was, and that was wonderful.

He leaned toward her.

Was he going to kiss her good-night? She held her breath as he wrapped his arms around her and gave her a hug. As they broke apart, he leaned down and kissed her forehead, then he glanced at his watch and said, "Thanks again, Sami. I've got to go."

Before she could respond, he'd turned around and headed down the porch stairs toward his car.

Well, that solved that. A kiss on the forehead was definitely not the way you ended a date. She'd just had dinner with an old friend.

And for some reason, Samantha was disappointed.

Chapter Five

"And he hasn't called me since. It's been a week and two days, not that I'm counting," Samantha reported to Michelle and Carly nine nights later at the general PTA meeting in the school cafeteria.

She pulled at the mock turtleneck, wishing she had worn something lighter. But this time of year in Erie, a day might start out cool and be in the seventies by lunch.

She hated to have this conversation with the other school parents milling about, but they had a table all to themselves and there were so many other conversations going on, no one seemed to be paying them the slightest bit of attention.

"I don't know what I did," she continued. "I thought it was a great evening. Obviously, I was wrong."

"Sam, it doesn't sound as if you did anything," Michelle assured her.

"I must have. I mean, who goes out with someone, but never calls them again?"

"Maybe Harry's not as over his past relationship as he thought," Carly suggested. "Men are not the most astute creatures ever."

"Or maybe he decided he was better off without

getting involved with me, even if that involvement was just a friendship."

"Sam." There was a mixture of sympathy and censure in Michelle's tone. "If he didn't see what a catch you were, he's not worth fretting about."

"The least he could have done was tell me it didn't work for him. A simple, *Hi, Sam. Sorry, things just didn't go as good for me as they went for you. I'll see you at the next PTA meeting.* How hard is that?" She felt a spurt of anger. She didn't deserve to be ignored. "I'll confess, I'm not quite sure how to act when I see him. I mean, is there a book on how to greet someone you had dinner with once? Well, three times, if you count the Saturday pizza and Sunday meat loaf with the kids."

"Samantha." There was urgency in Carly's voice. "I don't think we have time to plan a greeting with you. Here he comes. Don't let him see he's confused you."

Part of Samantha wanted to slink away and avoid talking to Harry Remington. But another part, a thankfully stronger part, squared her shoulders and did her best to maintain a calm facade.

"Ladies," Harry said, at his most affable.

Michelle and Carly didn't offer him a verbal response, but rather two identical curt nods. Samantha nodded, as well, and said, "Mr. Remington. Have a great meeting." Then she turned back to her friends, ignoring the fact he was still standing behind her. "Now, about the Thanksgiving Pageant," she said loudly, probably too loudly.

"He's gone." Carly was glaring in what, Samantha assumed, was Harry's direction.

"Stop giving him the evil eye, Carly. People are going to notice. And I don't want my humiliation to be fodder for the Erie Elementary gossip circles."

Gossip was what some mothers at the school lived on.

Who dumped who. Who dated who. Vying for best kids. My kid got an A…. My kid won a whatever…. Samantha had done her best to stay out of the gossip circles, both as a participant and as a topic.

"He's a sleaze," Carly hissed. "And I'm an expert at sleaze. I spent thirteen years married to my ex. Did I ever tell you what led to our divorce?"

Samantha knew this was Carly's attempt at distracting her, and she willing went along with it. "Well…"

"It was a couch."

"A couch led to your divorce?" Michelle asked.

Carly nodded. "I spent months shopping for a new couch to go in his office. I can't tell you how many stores I visited. After all that work, I finally found it, and when I went to the office to admire the complete redo, the couch didn't look the way I thought it would. I mean, I'd never envisioned it with him and his secretary naked on it."

"Oh, Carly." Samantha reached out and squeezed her friend's hand.

"Seriously, I'm okay now," Carly assured them. "It was just so cliché. But I'm over it. Well, I'm mainly over it. I even asked for the couch in our divorce settlement."

"What are you going to do with it? Sell it?" Michelle asked.

"Burn it. I'm going to set a match to it. A sort of cleansing. Out with the old life, in with the new."

Michelle looked as if she wasn't quite sure whether to believe Carly or not. Samantha didn't have that problem. The glint in Carly's eyes told her, her new friend meant to do exactly what she said she was going to do. She didn't want to encourage her, but she totally understood the sentiment. She'd been hurt when Phillip left her. Sad and embarrassed that their marriage had failed. But there'd been nothing like the white-hot fury she saw burning in Carly's eyes.

They listened to the PTA executives read and approve the minutes from the last meeting. Then the treasurer reported on the budget, pitched the next fund-raiser, and talked about upcoming events.

Despite her best intentions, Samantha kept finding herself looking at Harry sitting at the front table between Heidi and Mary Ann, the PTA treasurer.

He looked tired. There were dark circles under his eyes.

What if he'd been sick? He might not have felt up to a phone call. And truly, they'd been two school chums having dinner. He didn't really owe her a call. Maybe she'd owed him one? If she'd called the day after the dinner and thanked him... Yes, that's probably what she should have done. To call now would be awkward at best, so she wouldn't.

He'd been polite coming over to talk to her. Polite. That's what she was going to shoot for. She'd be another polite PTA mom, with no expectations or recriminations.

She made herself look away from Harry, and thought again about *How to Be Happy Without Really Trying.* To be optimistic was the first lesson, and she thought she'd made a lot of headway. To accept. Specifically, to accept her right to be happy, was the second.

Fine.

She'd accept that Harry had been a one-time dinner thing. Whenever she saw him next, she was going to behave like any other school parent.

She couldn't control the fact their dating hadn't worked out. She couldn't change it, and even if she could, she wouldn't try. She'd tried to hold on to Phillip, long after their relationship had failed, and that hadn't worked.

She was going to accept her right to be happy without a man. She'd managed the last year, she could continue to go it on her own as long as it took to find the right man.

Someone who would stick with her, no matter what.

And if she never found him, she'd stay single.

Samantha had learned that being alone was infinitely better than being with the wrong man.

HARRY REALIZED HE'D MADE a huge mistake.

He'd debated when he should call Samantha. He didn't know the protocol. He didn't want to move so fast that he made her feel smothered, but obviously he'd moved too slowly. He'd actually known after the third day, he'd moved too slowly.

Now what?

"And now that we've finished our PTA business, let me introduce tonight's speaker, Dr. Alison Addison. Her program's title is I Like You, Why Don't You Like Me? We'll be discussing cliques, bullying and childhood spats."

Harry forced himself to sit up straight and stare at some indistinct point on the wall, but what he really wanted to do was groan and lay his head down on the table.

He hazarded a glance at Samantha. Her two friends were shooting him eye-daggers, and Samantha was staring at some equally indistinct point on another wall of the cafeteria.

He'd sworn he'd never get involved with another mother. Now, he was adding an addendum, especially if she's a mother at his school. It didn't matter if it was dating or dinner, either way, he lost.

So, here he was again. Back in awkward-ville, all because he didn't listen to himself.

"…bullies, and even fights," Dr. Addison was saying.

"Children are social. They have trouble coping when one of their friends suddenly withdraws…"

The truth of the matter was, he'd been embarrassed by his confession at dinner. Yes, he'd loved Teresa and Lucas, and that relationship had failed. Those months right after she'd moved had been some of the hardest he'd ever gone through. It was even worse than when his parents had divorced.

He'd vowed then to never get involved with another mother, period. He'd missed out on having a real family twice. He wasn't going through it for a third time.

The only reason he'd even considered dinner with Samantha was that he was leaving town in a couple months. Two old friends who enjoyed each other's company, there was nothing wrong with that. And he knew, part of the reason he hadn't called was to prove he could *not* call her.

Well, he'd proven that.

"Sometimes there are underlying issues. Encouraging your child to talk to their friend…"

He'd talk to her and do his best to explain. He owed her that. He'd hurt her by not calling, he saw that tonight. And hurting Samantha had been the last thing he'd wanted to do.

Harry felt the urge to groan mounting to a previously unknown level.

How long could a PTA meeting possibly last?

"How much longer?" Samantha whispered to Michelle.

"You're worse than Brandon," she whispered back, but obliged Samantha and checked her watch. "Ten minutes, if she finishes on schedule."

With the way Samantha's luck was running, the

speaker was definitely going to go over. She'd probably talk for another half hour on rejection and abandonment.

Under normal circumstances, Samantha might have found the talk instructive, given her kids' situation, but because looking at the speaker meant looking in Harry's direction, she just wanted it over.

She wanted to go home, crawl in her bed and forget this particular PTA meeting ever happened.

"Thank you for inviting me this evening." The speaker sat down.

And perpetually perky Heidi popped up and said, "Thank you for such an interesting presentation, Doctor. I hope you stay and enjoy some refreshments with us. And I want to thank our eighth-grade parents. They won tonight's attendance award, so the eighth-grade class will have a jeans day on Friday. Thank you all for coming. Hope to see you again next month."

"I really should go," Samantha said. Tomorrow. She'd practice not avoiding him and being just another school mom tomorrow.

Carly shook her head. "No way. You'll get some refreshments, and if any single fathers pass our way, you're going to flirt."

"I don't flirt."

"Don't think of it as flirting," Carly said, draping an arm over Samantha's shoulder and leading her toward the line food and drinks. "Think of it as just making conversation…with style."

Michelle got in line behind them. "Carly, may I point out that you're as single as Samantha is, and I don't see you flirting with anyone here."

"We're all three in the same boat, remember? You're not flirting, either. And you're younger, so you should be flirting more."

"Ladies," Samantha said, feeling as if she were refereeing between two of her kids and seeing all hopes of fleeing evaporating. Fine. She'd stay and just hope Harry took her earlier bruskness as a hint to steer clear. "I don't think any of us is very flirty by nature. So, let's just grab a snack, then get out of here. I meant to tell you, there's no real reason to meet again on Friday, I really don't have much to do. Mrs. Tarbot has everything under control for the pageant. I'll go to a few rehearsals with the class and maybe help her with a couple of costumes."

"There may not be any Thanksgiving Pageant news to discuss, but I think we can all agree there's always kid stuff, or man stuff, or just life stuff," Carly said. "I'm beginning to rely on our meetings."

"Me, too," Michelle admitted. "That is if you don't mind…"

"No," Samantha quickly assured both of them. "Of course, I don't mind. I just wasn't sure if the two of you could spare the time every other week when the meetings aren't really necessary."

"Not necessary to the school activities, maybe, but definitely necessary to my mental health," Carly quipped.

"Great. It's a date," Samantha said, feeling relieved.

"A date?" came a distinctly male voice from behind them.

All three women turned in unison.

Harry stood there, looking less than happy.

"A date?" he repeated as he stared at Samantha, obviously waiting for a reply.

So much for steering clear. And the expression on his face said he didn't get that she was just another school mom.

Samantha got as far as saying, "Harry," when Carly

butted in, "Yes, a date. Samantha's a very desirable woman, and has men waiting for a chance to date her."

And before Samantha could tell Harry the truth, Carly pulled her back into the refreshment line.

"Sorry, Mr. Remington," Michelle murmured before she turned, as well.

Carly leaned across Samantha and whispered to Michelle, "What did you apologize to him for?"

Michelle also leaned in front of Samantha. "Because he looked a bit stricken."

"Serves him right," Carly said.

"Maybe I should go tell him—"

"Oh, no." Carly tightened her arm around Samantha's shoulders. "You let him stew on the knowledge that he's not the only man interested in you."

"We never established how deep his interest ran, and it obviously didn't run very deep," Samantha muttered.

"Then letting him think you're going out with someone else shouldn't be a problem."

"It's a lie," Michelle spoke quietly. "And lies are always a problem."

"Oh, no, she's one of those," Carly said to Samantha in mock horror.

"One of what?" Michelle eyed Carly suspiciously.

"An idealist. A young innocent who thinks the world is fair. If the world were, I'd have never found my husband and his secretary on my couch."

"I'm not as innocent as you think." Michelle wore an expression of someone far older than Samantha knew she was.

That's when Samantha rediscovered her voice. Using her best motherly tone, she said, "Okay, you two. Enough. Or no chocolate for either of you."

Both Carly and Michelle smiled.

"Oh, she's using her mean-mom voice." Carly didn't look the least bit intimidated.

"Is it working?" Samantha asked.

"Yeah." Michelle's grin said differently.

"Hey, I deal with four kids on a daily basis, I can handle you two." Samantha glanced behind her to find Harry who'd been cornered by three other PTA mothers, and for a moment he glanced up and their eyes locked. Then, as quickly as the connection happened, he broke off contact, and focused his attention on the women in front of him.

Fine. So, he didn't enjoy their date as much as she had. She'd get over it and move on.

Samantha had taken her first tentative steps into single life, and she stumbled. It didn't mean she couldn't get up and try again.

She deserved to be happy.

Samantha Williams wasn't going to let one bad date ruin her optimism.

IT DIDN'T TAKE A ROCKET scientist to realize that Samantha Williams was avoiding him.

The morning after the PTA meeting, Harry had called her house. He'd remembered that she had Tuesday mornings off. But either she was out running errands, or screening her calls, because he got the answering machine.

"Hi, Sami. I want to explain why I didn't call. Call me back?"

A few days later he called again. Stan picked up and when the boy asked who was calling, Harry didn't get any further than "Mr. Reming—" before the boy hung up on him.

The following week, he called on Wednesday after ten, hoping the kids were in bed and the house would be quiet. Samantha had answered with a rather frazzled, "Hello?"

Harry managed to spit out, "Samantha, it's Harry. I know you're mad that I didn't call after our date. It's not you, it's me. You see—"

That's as far as he got before there was a horrible yowl. He assumed it was the cat, not Samantha, but he was sure it was her who shouted, "Yes, of course, it is. I understand." There was another horrible yowl that he hoped was from the cat, not one of the kids. "I've got to go."

And she'd hung up.

He wondered who she'd gone out with? One of the fathers from the school? He knew there were a few single dads. Izzy Rizzo's dad for one. He'd seen the guy at the meeting. He was a lawyer or something. Harry hated thinking about the two of them out to dinner, or maybe a movie.

Today was Friday, and he'd sent her flowers. Periwinkles. The florist had said they meant friendship. Harry hadn't known that flowers had different meanings, but he liked the symbolism.

Samantha had sent them back.

He'd also never known you could return flowers, nonetheless the box of periwinkles arrived at his office. In place of his card, he received a note that said,

I get it, it's not me, it's you. It wasn't even a date, Harry, just a very nice dinner. It wasn't by any means a declaration of anything. Enough.

She hadn't even signed the note.

Why that bothered him, he didn't know.

He should be grateful. Samantha seemed to understand him.

Which made one of them.

He should have called her the day after their dinner and invited her out again.

He should have said something more at the PTA meeting.

Disgusted with himself, he took the box of flowers with him after school, and rather than driving home, drove to Samantha's house. The eastside neighborhood was an eclectic collection of homes. Small vinyl-sided Capes, two-story brick houses, and an occasional newer split-level or ranch style bungalow. Newer being relative. All the homes had an established, been around for decades sort of look. It was a cheery neighborhood in the autumn sunshine with the leaves littering the sidewalks.

It was three-thirty when he knocked on the door. It was brisk, despite the sunshine, and he wished he'd worn a jacket. He clutched the flowers and rang the bell.

He was startled as a foot appeared overhead on the trellis that framed the house's porch. The one blue sneakered foot was followed by a second, then jean-clad legs, then the edge of a black cape and finally, a masked face. Dark eyes widened when the masked figure spotted him.

"Mr. Rem?"

Harry was pretty sure he recognized the voice. "Seton?"

The masked head nodded. "You seen my brothers?"

"No. I know we're not at school now and I have no authority here, but really, the porch roof isn't a good place to play."

"But they've kidnapped Stella and I'm trying to rescue her."

Harry nodded. "That's very commendable, but you need to get off the roof."

The masked face bobbled up and down. "Okay, I'll go back into my room. Don't tell 'em you saw me if you see them."

"I won't tell them, but I'm going to have to tell your mom."

Even masked, Seton's panic was evident. "Oh, man, she's going to kill me."

Before Harry could try and assure Seton that his mother might yell, but that death was unlikely, the boy's feet disappeared. Harry could hear footsteps that abruptly stopped as he assumed Seton had climbed back into the bedroom. A loud thud told him he was right, and the boy had closed the window.

Just in time, because the front door opened. "Harry."

There was no smiled greeting only a frown on Samantha's face. "Did the kids do something at school?"

"No. But—"

She interrupted him. "Then we have nothing to talk about."

"Mmm, I could suggest that the fact Seton was on the roof might constitute something that should be discussed."

"I'll kill him." Discussion didn't seem to be high on Samantha's priority list, because without further commentary, she sprinted up the stairs, leaving the front door open.

Harry could have left. After all, Samantha had made herself clear about not wanting to see him again. He knew he should just leave the flowers and go. But knowing and doing were two different things. For instance, when he was young, he'd known throwing snowballs at cars wasn't smart, and yet he found himself doing it anyway. It was the same division between knowing and doing that led him to step into Samantha's foyer and close the door behind him.

"What have I told you about crawling out your window onto the porch?" he heard Samantha say upstairs.

Whatever Seton parroted back was low enough that Harry couldn't make it out. "Now, where are your siblings?" Pause. "You're right, it is noble to try and rescue your baby sister, but it's severely lacking in judgment to not listen to your mother's rules. And I have a very firm rule about climbing on roofs of any type. So, you sit in here and think about all my rules so you don't forget next time."

Pause.

"Yes, I'll go rescue Stella."

Pause.

"I am more than capable of taking on your brothers, but I do appreciate your offer to back me up. Unfortunately, you're imprisoned in this bedroom until further notice. Think about house rules until supper time."

Harry heard a door close and footsteps down the hall. Samantha came down the stairs, muttering to herself. She stopped abruptly when she spotted him. "You're still here."

"Yes." He held the florist's box out to her. "They put little plastic water bottles on the ends of the flowers, and then I put them in the fridge, so they should still be good. I want to—"

He actually thought she was going to argue, but she simply held out her hands, took the box and said, "I don't have time for any more apologies, I've been assured that Stella's life is hanging by a thread. I'm the only one who can save her. So, thanks for the flowers. It was snotty of me to send them back. All is forgiven, not that there was anything to forgive. Goodbye, Harry."

"Since Seton can't back you up, due to his current incarceration, maybe you'll permit me to help you save Stella?"

"I don't need anyone's help, Harry." She looked so

sure of herself. So ready to take on the world single-handedly. For a moment, he saw little Sami Burger.

"That's not what you said that first day in my office. You needed help with the boys."

"And you gave it. That was kind, and I appreciated it."

"So, let me help now. Then maybe we can talk."

"There's nothing to talk about. Though you're not going to leave, are you?"

He shook his head.

"Fine. You can help me with Stella, then you can leave with a guilt-free conscience."

"There are a few things I need to say."

"And I don't think there's any point."

"Samantha…"

However Samantha was already walking toward the back door. She set the flowers on the counter, before charging outside.

Harry was left with no other option but to follow her. He watched Samantha holler, "Stan and Shane, bring your sister and get in this house right now."

"I thought we were looking for them," he protested.

"I never said that. I said I'd rescue Stella, and I just did." She pointed to the far corner of the yard where the two boys emerged with Stella, who was blindfolded. "Boys, let your sister see, immediately."

They did, and all of them trooped into the kitchen. "I'm going to ask this just once. Was anyone else on the roof?" Samantha's tone was stern.

Shane nodded.

"You know that was wrong. March up to your room, have a seat on your bed and you think about what could have happened if you'd fallen. Think about the house rules and why we have them."

"You?" she asked Stan.

"I told him to get off, and I didn't let him take Stella out." He glared at Harry. "But I'll go to my room, too, and make sure they don't talk."

He followed his brother.

"And you?" Samantha asked Stella.

"I don't climb on roofes. I was the kidnapped princess, and Seton was my knight, trying to rescue me. But the boys put that scarf around my eyes, and I didn't like the game no more." She looked as if she was deciding whether she should cry, or simply go and whack her brothers.

"Why don't you see if watching a Disney movie will help you recover from your ordeal."

"A princess movie?" The potential tears evaporated at the idea of a brother-free princess-fest and Stella grinned.

"Yes."

As if noticing him for the first time, she said, "Hi, Mr. Rem," as she dashed away from them toward the living room.

"The boys don't generally let her watch princess movies. They're obsessed with sports and science-fiction shows."

He nodded. "Samantha—"

"Have a seat. While the boys are under house arrest, and Stella's bonding with a princess, you have the floor." She took one of the stools at the island, and nodded at the one next to it.

Suddenly, Harry couldn't think of what to say. "I wanted to say I'm sorry."

"Harry, you've said it, but we both know there's nothing to be sorry about. Two old friends went out for an evening. A very nice evening, I might add. There were no expectations on either of our parts. You're leaving in a few months anyway, remember?"

She was letting him off the hook, but rather than feeling relieved, he felt worse. "But I should have called."

"Seriously, Harry, no, you shouldn't have. It's all good. It was just a dinner."

"That's what I've told myself, but you and I both know it wasn't just a dinner like you'd have with Mrs. Lewis and Miss Hamilton. It was more. And when I heard you were going out with someone else—"

"Going out with someone else?" Samantha looked genuinely perplexed.

"Your date?"

"My what?"

"At the PTA meeting, your friends said something about your *date*."

"Oh, that." She laughed.

"Yeah, that. I just wanted to say, he's a lucky man, whoever he is."

"Yes, whoever."

There was something going on here, but Harry wasn't sure exactly what. "You're helping at the Halloween party?"

"Yes."

"Then I'll see you there. I should be going." He waited, hoping she'd ask him to stay, but she didn't. Reluctantly, he walked out of the kitchen and into the living room, on his way to the front door, Samantha following on his heels.

"Mr. Rem, do you like *Mulan?*" The little girl had a number of DVD cases spread out in front of her. She held the one that proclaimed *Mulan* aloft.

"I've never seen *Mulan,* Stella."

"Oh, Mr. Rem, that's too bad." She looked stricken on his behalf. "The boys say it's one of the best princess movies, 'cause she fights and she's not really a princess, but I think she is." Stella paused a moment, and her expression lightened. "You can watch it with me now, if you like."

"I—" He looked from the little girl to her mother. Samantha shrugged her shoulders.

"Please?" Stella begged. "You'll like it."

"Stella, Mr. Remington probably has other things to do with his afternoon."

"To be honest, I don't have anything else to do with my afternoon. And unless it's a problem with you, I'd very much like to watch the movie with Stella. It's important for school officials to stay in touch with the kids they work with."

"Harry, I'm not sure I understand what you're doing."

"Neither do I. If I did, I'd explain it. All I know is that I'd like to stay, with your permission."

He thought she was about to tell him it was indeed a problem for her, but the moment passed and she said, "Suit yourself, then."

HARRY HAD TAKEN HER AT her word, Samantha realized an hour and a half later. He'd finished watching *Mulan* with Stella, but rather than leaving, he'd gone with Seton and Shane—released from their room—to inspect the latest updates to the clubhouse the boys had built in the backyard.

Samantha glanced at the three of them, traipsing across the lawn, and disappearing into the woods. Well, they weren't really "woods," but that's what the boys called the small copse of trees that lined the back of their lot.

The boys had assembled the clubhouse on their own, buying the lumber with their allowances. It was small, but they'd enjoyed working on it as their summer project.

"Mom, is it Saturday?" Stella glanced out the kitchen window into the backyard.

She'd felt left out, so the boys instituted a Saturdays-for-Stella rule. She got to be an honorary member only one day a week. That, along with the small play-tent Samantha had bought for her, had kept her happy.

"No, Stella. It's Friday. Tomorrow's Saturday."

"Oh." But without a pause, she sprinted through the kitchen, out the backyard, across the lawn and into the clubhouse.

Stan thumped into the kitchen, and sat at the counter. Samantha continued drying the glass in her hand, and waited.

"I don't know why he's here again," her son finally said.

She didn't have to ask who *he* was. She also didn't mention that she didn't know why Harry was here, either.

"We don't need no new guy," he continued. "We have a dad."

"Who'll be here at seven to pick you up." She looked at her obviously upset son. "You think that's what Harry wants? To be your dad?"

"Yeah."

"Stan, honey, no one—not Mr. Remington, not anyone—can ever replace your dad. You have a father who loves you."

"He didn't love us for the year he hardly ever saw us."

The pain in Stan's voice almost floored her. She'd do just about anything to be able to have spared him that. "Stan, you're old enough to understand your father was going through something. I can't pretend to understand what it was, but that doesn't change the fact that he was having a problem. He told you, told all of us, he'd been seeing a doctor, trying to work it out. It wasn't you, and it wasn't me. It was your dad's problem. And he seems to be getting better. He's back and he's trying."

"'Cause Lois made him come back."

When Phillip had walked out on her, she'd never imagined that there would come a day when she would defend him, but tonight she'd do just that. "Stan, your father and I were friends before we ever got married, and I think now that we're not married, we're finding out we're still able to be friends. I can guarantee you that no matter how much he loves Lois, no one ever made your father do anything. Phillip Williams is a man who sorts things out on his own."

"Yeah, I guess."

"And even if he had some problems last year that doesn't mean he didn't love you. It means he trusted me enough to look out for all of you until he could again."

"You guys are really still friends?" Stan didn't look as if he quite believed it.

Samantha couldn't fault him—it surprised her, as well. Oh, maybe *friends* was a fairly broad definition, but it was close. "I think so."

"And now he's got a girlfriend, but that doesn't bother you?"

Samantha didn't answer right away. She reflected for a few seconds. "Stan, I can honestly say I wish your father all the happiness in the world. If that's with Lois, then no, she doesn't bother me."

"'Cause you don't love him anymore, right?"

Sensing there was more to the question, Samantha replied, "Stan, are you worried that because your father and I stopped loving each other, we'll stop loving you?" Before he could respond, she continued, "Because I can assure you, that will never happen. Even when your father took some time away, it wasn't that he didn't love you, it was that he had to straighten out his own life before he could come back into yours."

He didn't meet her eyes, so she gently took his chin and made him look up. "Stan, I love you. Nothing could change that. Ever. You're my son."

"What if you start dating some guy who didn't like us kids?"

"That's an easy answer… I'd dump him. And let me point out, Lois likes you. She's encouraging your father to see more of you. Your father and I both love you, and everyone else is secondary to that. If there's nothing else you believe in life, believe that."

Stan didn't say anything, but nodded. "That's what that school shrink Mr. Remington made us see said."

"She was right."

The moment wasn't just broken, it was shattered by the kids running back into the kitchen.

"Mom, Mom, Mr. Rem had a great idea for the club-house. The tree has that one high branch. He said he could put a swing in it, if it was okay with you," Seton said in one long breath.

"I told 'em it would be okay," Shane added.

"But he said we had to ask you. Please, Mom."

"Yeah, please?"

Harry and Stella came in as the boys finished their plea.

"Sorry. I was talking about my old clubhouse and…" He looked rueful. "The boys promised to live with your response, no begging or recriminations if you said no."

Four faces looked at her, waiting for her response, only Stan didn't offer her a pleading look. He purposely was staring anywhere but at her.

"Are you sure it would be safe?" Samantha asked.

Harry nodded. "The branch is plenty big enough to support any of them."

"Then I guess a swing would be a great addition."

"And it's not in the clubhouse, so I can use it even if it's not a Stella Saturday, right?"

"Right," Harry and Samantha both automatically agreed.

Seton and Shane seemed as if they might object, but when they saw the look in Samantha's eyes they must have thought better of it. "Right," they echoed.

"Mr. Rem, when can you put it up?" Stella asked.

"Tomorrow, if that works for your mom."

The kids all stared at her. She was trapped. "The kids' father has them this weekend. He's coming around seven to get them."

"Maybe next weekend then?" Harry asked.

Samantha could sense the kids were anxious for her to accept. Even if she wanted to, there was nothing to do but say, "Fine. Next Saturday."

"You're sure?" Harry asked, as the three younger children excitedly chattered, and Stan continued to scowl.

"Positive. And I guess, if you were here around one, I'd probably feed you before you had to go to your class."

"You can bet I'll be here."

"You're not going to ask what we're having?"

"It doesn't matter. But if the kids are going to their dad's for the weekend at seven, I should probably let you get things ready. It's almost six."

Harry walked to the door, and Samantha followed. He turned sharply and drew a breath. "I got scared, Sam. It's that plain and simple. The dinner went well, and I can't remember when I've had so much fun. I kept trying to convince myself it was only a dinner, but it was a date. A great date. So, rather than calling and going out again, I froze. I meant it when I said, it wasn't you, it was me."

"I'm pretty sure that phrase is generally considered the kiss of death." Samantha offered him a smile to let him know she was teasing.

"This time, it's simply the truth."

"You didn't call because you enjoyed dinner so much."

"When you say it that way, it sounds stupid." He kissed her forehead. "Did I totally blow it, or can we go out again?"

"Before we do, tell me, Harry, what do you want?" He seemed startled by the question, so she added, "Because I'll tell you what I want. Right now, my focus is on my kids, seeing that they recover from the divorce. And we seem to be heading in that direction. They're better. So, what I want is a man who's not looking for a commitment. Someone who will spend time with me, share a few grown-up conversations. A friend. Someone who isn't looking for a romance, because, Harry, I'm not. I'm not sure if I'll ever be looking in that direction again. And it's not that I'm jaded, that I don't believe in love. I do. I just don't have time for it. I've got work and my kids, even volunteering at the school. A relationship isn't in the cards, at least not now. So, if we did try again, I want to be up front about what I want. It would be casual all the way. That's the way it would have to be. The question is…what do you want, Harry?"

"I want to see you again. I want talk to you. To laugh with you. Whether we're here with your kids, or out by ourselves, I want to spend time with you. But you're right, I'm not looking for anything serious, especially not with someone who has kids."

She must have appeared as shocked as she felt, because he added, "I can't do it again, Sam. I've always dreamed of a family, but I've lost two. The first when my parents divorced, and I'll confess, that sounds lame even to me, but it's how I feel. Then there was the family I'd built with Teresa and Lucas. I can't raise a kid as mine, but have no rights, and have him ripped away. So, as much as I want to spend time with you, it has to be casual for me, as well. Just friends."

"So, we've established ground rules. We're not dating, but we are going to see one another. Platonically," she added for clarity. "So, in the interest of seeing one another, why don't you come over next weekend and hang a swing, and we'll go from there."

"Sounds good." He started to walk away. "If I were to call you this week, would you answer?"

"Probably," she said, knowing she was wearing a goofy grin.

Harry nodded. "Good. I'll talk to you later."

Samantha watched him go and smiled. His confession thawed something in her. Harry was just as confused as she was. He was coming out of a long-term relationship, too.

A platonic friendship. And he was leaving in two months anyway.

That made him safe.

Maybe it was cowardly, but safe was all she needed right now.

Chapter Six

It occurred to Harry that he'd fallen into the rhythm of not dating Samantha. The tree swing had been a huge success, and he'd seen her almost every night since.

He didn't worry about protocols, didn't worry about when it was too soon to call. There was no too soon. He'd leave her house and find himself putting on his Bluetooth so he could talk to her on the drive home.

If the kids were home and still awake, the conversations were invariably interesting, punctuated with things like, "No. Don't you dare put Grunge in the dryer. It wouldn't be anything like a carnival ride," or "Boys, what did I say about using beds as trampolines, especially my bed? ...Yes, I know it's the biggest bed in the house, but still, no jumping."

Today marked a week since the tree swing, and the whole Williams family was going to the Erie Elementary Halloween party with him. It was the perfect day for it. The trees had reached their peak colors. The sky was blue, with puffy white clouds alternately hiding or framing the sun. The air had moved beyond crisp to downright chilly.

He glanced over at Samantha, sitting in the passenger seat of his red Ford Expedition. He'd bought the

SUV when he and Teresa were still together. It had made hauling Lucas and his friends around a piece of cake.

Thinking of Lucas dimmed Harry's mood. This was the first of Lucas's Halloweens he was missing. When Lucas called last night, he'd spent a half hour talking about his cool vampire costume. "I've even got fake blood." Harry had been suitably impressed, and made all the right responses. He'd done just fine, until Lucas ended the conversation with, "I wish you were taking me trick-or-treating." That's when the pain had hit.

Harry forced himself to set last night's call aside and concentrate on today. He was thankful that he'd kept the SUV when he'd moved to Erie. He'd thought about trading it in before he left Columbus, but remembered that in Erie winter came early and sometimes hit with a vengeance; he'd decided to wait until he got home to get another smaller car. He was glad of it now. The third row of seating meant he could fit the entire Williams family in.

"Mr. Rem, can I sit in the back on the way home?" Stella asked from her middle-seat position.

"That was the deal. Everyone has to trade off."

"See?" she called triumphantly to Shane and Seton, the current backseat residents.

"This will only take me a minute," he promised Samantha as he turned onto Grandview Boulevard.

"Harry, it's fine. Go get your camera. We'll only be a few blocks out of our way, and the Halloween party will be there when we get there."

He pulled into the condo's driveway, and slammed on the breaks with a jerk. There was another vehicle in his parking spot.

A familiar vehicle.

His mother's vehicle.

Things had been going so well with Erie Elementary,

his classes and not dating Samantha, he'd been feeling upbeat. But at the sight of the car, his spirits plummeted. This could not be good. If his mother had made the four-hour drive from Columbus to Erie without even checking to see what his schedule was, she was on a mission. He could almost feel the bull's-eye on his forehead.

He saw her coming and felt the urge to hum the tune to *Jaws*. "Sami, I'm sorry."

"Harry, what is it?"

"Harry?" came a high, happy voice.

"Just know I'm sorry in advance," he whispered to Samantha. "It's my mom."

"Harry, don't be silly, I'm sure it's fine."

Knowing his mother, he knew it wasn't. There was that particular gleam in her eye. The one she'd worn when he was ten and didn't want braces, and she made him. It said, "I'm doing this for your own good." He just wasn't sure what *this* was yet.

He loved his mom. Adored her actually. However, unannounced visits from Marilyn George were never good things. Not by any stretch of the imagination.

"Surprise," she said as he approached. His mom was still a very attractive lady. She'd never dyed her hair, but rather than making her seem old, the white hair mixed in streaks with her dark hair looked striking.

Striking. That was the best way to describe his mother. Harry didn't know anything about designer clothes, but he knew that his mother's pantsuit wasn't inexpensive. Her haircut and makeup were just so. She was still a beautiful woman, he realized with a sense of pride, although the determined expression she wore made him nervous. "Mom, I wish you'd called. I have an engagement today."

"With the woman in the car?" His mom peered into the car, her curiosity evident.

"That's Samantha. She's an old friend. Her kids attend Erie Elementary. We're all going to the school's Halloween party."

"Harry…" There was a flash of something akin to pain on her face, but the next second it was gone and she smiled. "A Halloween party, you say?"

"At the school. For the families."

"Now, isn't that a coincidence. You're the principal, which makes you part of the school, and we're your family, so of course, we'd love to go."

"We're…?" he asked.

"You stepfather is in the car."

Harry hadn't even noticed that there was someone in the passenger side. He waved, and his stepfather, Allen George, waved back. "You both came up?"

"Yes. We were hoping to spend some time with you. And a Halloween party is a good way to start. I remember how it goes at schools, they always need volunteers."

He couldn't think of any way out of it. He knew his mother well enough to guess that she wouldn't be talked out of coming to the party. As a matter of fact, odds were she'd be running the whole thing within moments of arriving. "Uh, do you want to follow me, then?"

"I might have moved from Erie years ago, but I can still get around. I remember where it is from here."

"Fine. I guess I'll see you there. I've just got to get my camera." He hurried in and retrieved it from the hook by the door, and came out, expecting his mother to be gone. Instead, she was waiting for him, and rather than heading to her own car, she followed him to his. "Hi, I'm Marilyn, Harry's mother. And you are…?"

Samantha smiled. "Samantha Williams. I was Sami Burger back then. I remember you from school, ma'am. You haven't changed a bit."

"You went to Erie Elementary?"

"I was two years behind Harry."

"Well, it's nice to see you again, dear. Maybe we can find a minute to catch up at the Halloween party?"

Samantha nodded. "I'd like that."

Harry was desperate to let Samantha know that if she spent that minute with his mom, Marilyn would pump her for information with all the finesse of a secret agent interrogating a suspect.

"And who do we have here?" his mom asked Stella.

"I'm Princess Stella, and that's Stan, Seton and Shane."

"And do all of you go to Erie Elementary?"

Stella nodded. "Mr. Rem's our principal."

"And I'm Mr. Rem's mom. You can call me Mrs. George." His mom looked at him with quiet speculation in her eyes. "I guess I'll see you all at the party." She waved and hurried back to her own car.

"And that was my mom," Harry said, feeling resigned. He got in the car and took off, cursing himself for forgetting his camera this morning. Otherwise, he wouldn't have known about his uninvited company until tonight.

"Is something wrong?" Samantha asked.

"I don't know. I don't know why she's here."

"She's your mother, Harry. She's here because she loves you. You've been away from home for two months. She probably just wanted to check on you. That's how mothers are."

He knew Samantha was right. His mother did love him. But he wasn't sure she'd ever really understood him. And he wasn't sure she'd ever really gotten over him refusing to leave his grandparents house when she remarried.

"Yes, she loves me, but…well, be prepared."

"For what?"

"She's seen you, and even now, she's trying to

analyze what that means. She won't understand not-dating dates."

"What's a not-dating date?" Stella asked.

Samantha turned around. "It means, Mr. Rem and I are just friends."

Harry didn't need to turn around and identify who snorted their disbelief. Stan's animosity was clear.

Harry was driving, so he didn't see what Samantha did, but he guessed it was one of those mom-looks because Stan immediately mumbled, "Sorry."

"Well, it's nice that your family can come to the party." Samantha was using the same tone she'd used when she'd tried to convince the kids to try a spinach quiche the other night. It hadn't worked then, either. He and Samantha had eaten the quiche. The kids ate hot dogs. "It's going to be fun."

Harry snorted this time, and at that moment, he knew how Stan had felt because Samantha gave him a look. It wasn't quite a mom-look, but he recognized it as saying she didn't approve of his rudeness.

"Sorry," he mumbled.

"Let's all be optimistic," Samantha ordered. When no one replied, she said, "It's going to be a great day."

Harry didn't dare snort again, but he gave Samantha a look that said he didn't have enough optimism to believe her.

SAMANTHA LOVED FALL, and Halloween was a favorite holiday. Last night, the kids had gone trick-or-treating, and today at the party, there would be apple bobbing, Fuhrman cider and Mighty Fine donuts. And just like every year, they'd have pin the tail on the black cat.

She watched as her kids piled out of Harry's SUV. Stella was dressed as a princess. She'd found an old spring-green prom dress at the thrift store, cut it down for Stella, then bought a dime-store tiara.

The boys were dressed in regular clothes. The upper grades were too cool for childish endeavors and no longer wore costumes. She couldn't get over how fast the kids were growing. In another three years, Stella wouldn't be dressing up, either.

The kids all hurried into the school. "Would you rather I waited with you, or should I just go in?" she asked Harry.

"You don't mind waiting?"

She smiled. "No. Not at all. I'm on apple-bobbing duty. After last year's near drowning, everyone realizes that it's a hazardous job. I can use a few more minutes to psych myself up for it."

"Almost drowning?" Harry asked.

"Bobby Brandt. He was determined to get an apple and held his breath so long that he accidentally inhaled the water, then…" She didn't finish the story because Harry's mother and stepfather were approaching them.

"Here goes," Harry muttered.

"Hello again, Mrs. Remington." Samantha caught her mistake. "I'm sorry. Mrs. George," she substituted, using the last name Harry's mom had introduced herself with.

"That's all right," Harry's mom said, looking not the least bit bothered. "This is my husband, Allen. Honey, this is Samantha Williams, formerly little Sami Burger. She went to school here at Erie Elementary back when Harry went here."

"It's nice to meet you." Allen George was a comfortable-looking man. He had a well-worn pair of jeans, slightly scuffed brown loafers and a soft-looking flannel shirt that spoke of numerous washings. He had salt-and-pepper hair, muddy grey eyes and a beard that lent a sort of Santa Clausish air to his appearance. "So, I understand we're having a Halloween party?"

Samantha nodded. "It's a school event and I'm on apple-bobbing duty, so I really should get in and help. I just wanted to say hi to you again, Mrs. George, and meet you, Mr. George."

Maybe she could stave off the interrogation Harry had warned her about.

Mrs. George smiled.

Samantha saw a look in Mrs. George's eyes that said there'd be no getting out of their little *catch up,* so she bowed to the inevitable. "I'll see you inside."

"Great." That settled, Harry's mother turned to him. "Now, Harry, give us a tour of the school?"

Harry nodded, and immediately his mother led him into the building. He turned and shot Samantha a little wave.

She followed them, but instead of heading up the stairs to Harry's office, she went down toward the cafeteria and the party.

There was one word that always worked to describe any type of party that included children...*chaos.*

And chaos reigned supreme today.

The cafeteria was decorated with orange-and-black streamers, pumpkins and a wide array of ghoulish figures. Princesses, pirates and a multitude of other costumed children ran from one activity to the next.

Samantha found the apple-bobbing booth, where Michelle and Carly waited for her. "I thought you both were at the face-painting booth?"

"When Heidi saw our first attempts, we were banished." Carly lowered her voice and confessed, "I botched it on purpose. Jonathan Byers was in my line, and last year, he barfed three times. He'd already been through the donut-on-a-rope game twice, so I wasn't taking any chances."

Michelle appeared to be trying to adopt a stern look, but her grin kept peeking through and ruining the effect. "I don't have an artistic bone anywhere in my body. My sister got all those genes." As if realizing what she'd said, a look of sorrow passed over her face.

"How long's it been now, honey?" Carly asked.

"Four years." She stopped and considered a moment. "Almost five years since she died and Brandon came to live with me. More than that since we lived together. It doesn't matter that we hadn't been close. Just knowing she was out there was enough. Just like knowing that now she's not hurts at the weirdest times."

Samantha reached over and gave Michelle a hug. She didn't say anything because she knew nothing she said would lessen Michelle's pain. Sometimes just being there was the best you could do.

"Thanks," Michelle said. "But we have a line."

The next hour went by in the blink of an eye. Samantha was soon thoroughly damp from various children emerging from the water and splashing her. She didn't mind. Everyone's spirits were high, and there were no near drownings.

"I thought I'd try my hand at bobbing for apples," mentioned Harry.

The kids in the vicinity clapped and started to gather at the booth.

Samantha looked around. Michelle and Carly had quickly disappeared to where they were unloading more apples for the barrel, leaving her to help Harry. Carly looked up and grinned, giving Samantha a small thumbs-up sign.

Knowing there was nothing to do about it, Samantha said to Harry, "Well, you know what to do." She turned to the kids who'd gathered. "Do you want to see if Mr. Remington can get an apple?"

Some of the kids screamed, "Yes," some clapped, but all made it obvious that they'd be delighted to see their principal get soaked trying to catch one of the buoyant fruits.

He made a big flourished to-do, removing his jacket and cuffing his sleeves before he walked up to the plastic bucket. "You're enjoying this," he whispered to Samantha.

"Maybe just a little," she answered with a grin. Louder, she said, "Okay, Principal Remington. Why don't you show the kids how a pro does it."

He plunged his entire head into the bucket so far the collar of his shirt was soon soaked. Seconds ticked by as he moved his head about, apparently chasing after his apple. Soon, he popped up, apple secure in his teeth.

The kids all clapped, and formed a line behind him for their turn. Michelle and Carly reappeared, taking over the apple-booth duty. "Why don't you get Principal Remington a towel?" Carly asked with all the subtlety of a brick.

Samantha gave Carly a look that she frequently subdued her kids with, but it only made her irrepressible friend grin.

Shaking her head, she grabbed a towel for Harry and also grabbed his jacket for him as he toweled off.

"It's been a long time since I bobbed for an apple." His voice was muffled under the towel.

"Well, you'd never know it. You got one the first time."

"Remember Mr. Constantine and his unfortunate apple-bobbing incident?"

"I remember him, but not the apple-bobbing incident." He was the grandfather of Jossette Constantine, a girl who was three years older than Samantha, one year older than Harry.

"I was in maybe second or third grade when we had a Halloween party with apple bobbing. Mr. Constantine bobbed for an apple, and that's when we learned that he was bald."

"You didn't notice before?" she asked.

"No. And we wouldn't have noticed then, either, but his toupee fell off in the water. It seems he forgot that he had it on."

Samantha laughed at the mental image. "Oh, the poor man. He must have been so embarrassed."

"Not him. He took the wet toupee and placed it on one of the pumpkins to dry." Harry finished with the towel and reached for his jacket.

His fingers grazed hers. Just the slightest touch. And yet, Samantha felt a sense of breathlessness. "Glad you didn't have to worry about that." It sounded lame to her ears, but she was feeling so flustered, it was the best she could do. "I better go help Carly and Michelle."

"And I better get back to circulating." Before he left, he said, "How 'bout I buy you a hot chocolate when your shift is done."

"That would be lovely."

She watched as he moved through the gym, on to the next booth. He'd picked the apple up and took a large bite as he walked. She wasn't sure why, but the action was endearing. He turned and waved. She returned the wave before turning back to her friends.

"Samantha's got a boyfriend," Carly whispered, grinning from ear to ear.

"Carly, it's not nice to tease," Michelle admonished, though she was grinning, as well.

"Okay, grow up, you two." Samantha didn't bother offering a lengthy explanation about how she and Harry were not dating. Judging from the smiles her two friends were still sporting, it wouldn't do any good.

She continued to assist with the apple bobbing, feeling remarkably bubbly.

"Who's the lady eyeing you?" Carly whispered, nodding her head. "She looks a bit long-in-the-tooth to be a mom."

"She is a mom…Harry's."

"Oh." There was an ominous tone to Michelle's voice. It sounded like Seton's *oh* last week when she'd warned him to leave the cookies alone until after supper. It had caused her to look up and notice the chocolate already adhering to the corners of his mouth.

"What do you mean, *oh?*"

Michelle whispered again, "I mean, she's scoping you out."

"I'm sure she isn't. It's not like Harry and I are an item." That had been her refrain so far and she was sticking to it.

Carly scoffed, and Michelle shot her a sympathetic look.

"Really. Harry and I are only friends," she told them for the umpteenth time.

"We're just friends," Carly pointed out, "but you don't call me half a dozen times a day, and spend almost every evening with me."

"I don't—"

"At our last meeting you took no less than three calls from him. And that was in under two hours. I think half a dozen is probably underestimating. You two are an item."

"We're not."

"Don't tell me," Carly said. "Tell her."

"Hi, Samantha." Harry's mom had stepped up to the booth, next to the line of children waiting their turns.

"Hi, again, Mrs. George."

"Call me Marilyn."

Using her first name felt awkward, so Samantha avoided it by not calling her anything. "Are you enjoying revisiting Erie Elementary?"

Rather than answer Samantha's questions, Harry's mom turned to Michelle and Carly. "I wonder if you two ladies would mind if I borrowed Samantha for a few minutes."

"No problem," Michelle said, shooting Samantha a helpless, what-else-could-I-say look.

"Sure, we can handle the kids," Carly added.

"Really, I should—" Samantha began.

"It will only take a minute," Mrs. George interrupted.

Samantha followed her as she wove through the throng. Mrs. George went to the first floor and let herself into Harry's office. "Ah, that's better. A bit of quiet." She sat down on the couch on one end of Harry's office and patted the seat next to her.

Samantha sat, not because she wanted to get all up close and cozy, but because she didn't have any other polite option. "Is there something that I can do for you, ma'am?"

"Marilyn."

"Marilyn," Samantha repeated, though the word felt sticky on her tongue.

"Harry says you're divorced and, as I saw, you have four kids?"

"Yes." She wasn't sure what she'd been expecting, but this wasn't it. "Yes. Stan's in eighth grade, Seton's in seventh, Shane's in sixth and Stella broke that every-year run and is only in third."

"And it's recent? The divorce, I mean," she clarified. "You've divorced recently?"

Samantha didn't appreciate the cross-examination, but she wasn't sure how to extricate herself from Harry's mother, so she answered slowly, "It's been a little more than a year now."

"I see." Mrs. George nodded and continued, "And Harry says you two are just friends? That you're not dating?"

"That's right."

"Listen, Samantha, I remember you as a little girl, but I realize I don't know much about you now. But I do know my son. Harry is still getting over his own breakup. Did he tell you that?"

"Yes. I know about Teresa."

"And Lucas," Mrs. George stressed.

"Yes, and him, too. Harry and I've talked."

"My son doesn't think I know him, but I know him better than he knows himself. And I'm not sure if he can handle another failed relationship, especially one where kids are involved."

"Mrs. George—"

"You see," Mrs. George interrupted, "for all intents and purposes, Lucas was his son. And you've never met a more devoted father. Lucas was only three when Harry and Teresa got together. He was there for all the ups and downs. He gave that little boy his heart, every bit as much as he gave it to Teresa. When she and Lucas left—"

"Ma'am." Samantha didn't know what to say. She sensed Marilyn George's pain on her son's behalf. "Harry and I *are* just friends."

"Yes, well, that's what you both say, but I've watched him look at you when he was bobbing for apples at your booth. There's more than friendship there. You can try to fool yourselves, but I'm not buying it." She sounded almost angry. She visibly got herself under control, and added, more softly, "I know my son, and I know it's… I don't want to see him hurt again."

"I'm not sure what you want me to say. I like Harry. He makes me laugh. For the first time in a long time, I'm happy. And before you tell me my happiness can't rely on someone else, that's not it. I was working my way back to happy on my own and Harry was there, waiting on the other side." As she said the words she realized they were true.

"I don't want either of you hurt," Mrs. George repeated.

"I don't want either of us hurt. The fact is Harry's leaving after Thanksgiving. He's got a life back in Columbus with you. He's got friends and a job there. Our friendship has an expiration date in December. We're both aware of that. There's no worries."

"I'm a mother, worrying is what I do best." She offered Samantha a smile, one that said she knew Samantha understood.

"I really should get back to the booth and help my friends." She glanced at her watch.

Mrs. George nodded. "I'm sorry, dear. I liked you when you were young, and I'm sure I'd like you as much now, if we had more time to spend together. It wasn't my place to say anything, but Harry's my son, and I don't want him to make the same mistakes."

"I promise I'll do everything I can to see to it that he doesn't get hurt."

"If you mean that, break it off with him now, while you're both still able to say it's just a friendship."

Samantha didn't know what to say to that, so she simply said, "I really need to go."

Harry's mom remained silent. She didn't make any move to follow Samantha as she practically sprinted from the office toward the gym.

She was in such a hurry she didn't even notice Harry until she'd practically run him down.

"What's the rush?" he asked.

"I've got to get back to my booth."

"Okay. See you in a bit."

"Yeah. See you."

Earlier, Carly had singsonged, *Samantha's got a boy-friend.*

Now, Harry's mother was accusing her of looking at Harry in a certain smitten way. She was going to have to be careful not to give them any more ideas. It was a shame that women in the new millennium were unable to understand that a man and a woman could be friends. Just friends.

She was all business when she returned to the apple-bobbing kids.

"Everything all right?" Michelle asked.

"Sure. Why wouldn't it be?"

Her two friends' expressions said they weren't really buying her assurances, but she didn't have the energy to try and explain. She was still too busy mulling over Mrs. George's words.

Maybe she was walking a dangerous path with Harry. If she were honest, there'd been moments that were more than friendly and possibly right next to flirting.

Samantha was no closer to resolving things when Harry dropped her and the children at home. Thankfully, in the car, the kids had kept the conversation light. Stella especially was babbling about the party, and last night's trick-or-treating with her father and Lois.

"Call you later," Harry said, more than asked.

"Okay. But if you're busy with your mom and stepdad, don't worry about it."

He gave her a quizzical look, but she just offered him her best smile and herded the kids into the house.

Stan was quiet. Too quiet. As the children all ran to their rooms to add today's treats to the myriad of candy they'd brought home this morning from their father's, Samantha called after her eldest. "Hey, Stan, give me a minute, would you?"

He turned and headed toward her. "What?"

"Is something wrong? You haven't been the same ever since Harry picked us up."

Instead of answering, he countered her question with, "Why'd we have to go with him?"

Samantha resisted the urge to sigh. She'd hoped their last conversation had helped Stan realize that Harry wasn't a threat, but obviously, it hadn't. So she tried again. "Because Harry's a friend and he asked us. We'd planned to go out to dinner afterward, except his parents showed up and he felt he should spend time with them."

"They're not his parents. It's his mom and her husband."

"Mr. Remington's stepfather." Stan looked as if there was definitely something more than a dislike of Harry.

"Yeah, but the guy's not Mr. Rem's father, and Mr. Rem's not my father."

"Stan, I know that. We've been through this. Harry knows that—"

"No, you don't. We all went to that stupid Halloween party together, walking in like some big happy family, but we're not, and we're never gonna be."

"Harry's just a friend," she said weakly, not sure what to do in the face of all Stan's anger.

"And Lois is just Dad's friend. You know us kids

didn't ask for this. We didn't want to have you two get a divorce."

No one asked me, either, Samantha wanted to cry. *Your father didn't ask as he packed his bags and left. There was no discussion. No huge disagreement—a moment I can point to and say that's what broke us. He just left, saying I'm not happy. Well, I'm not happy he's gone, Stan. I'm not happy that the life I thought I had was merely a sham.*

Oh, yes, that's what a part of her wanted to shout. To spew all the pain and confusion, letting it flow like lava, hot and bubbling, disgorging itself until all that pain was gone.

But this was her son—her very confused son. He didn't need her hurt on top of his own. He needed her to explain why his world had shifted.

They'd had this discussion previously, and Samantha would simply continue to say the words over and over again until they sank in. When he was little she'd repeated rules like look-both-ways-before-you-cross-the-street, don't-talk-to-strangers and eat-your-vegetables. To the best of her knowledge, he did look both ways, didn't talk to strangers and most of the time managed to eat his vegetables. She'd keep hammering this new point home as often as he needed to hear it.

"Stan, I love you. Your dad loves you. But the truth is, we didn't love each other anymore."

"How do you just stop loving someone?"

She hugged him. For a moment, he squirmed. He'd long since decided he was too old for such sympathetic displays from his mom. Most of the time she honored his wishes, but she knew he needed her touch. He needed to feel connected to her. She willed him to feel her love wrapping him as snugly as her arms were.

She repeated another variation of what she'd said the last time. "Stan, I wish I could explain it to you, because maybe then I'd understand it myself. Your dad and I were both so young when we married. People change and grow. And rather than growing together, we grew apart. Neither of us planned it. Neither of us wanted to hurt the other. I do love your dad, like a friend. I'm not sure exactly what's in store for either of us. Heck, I'm not even sure what I'm going to make for dinner tonight. But for all that I'm not sure about, for all I don't know, I can absolutely guarantee you that I'm positive about one thing—your dad and I will never stop loving you. Not ever."

"But I want us to be a family again." For all that Stan was thirteen—going on fourteen—there was still a little boy's longing in his words.

It tore at Samantha.

"Honey, we are a family. We'll always be a family, albeit a different kind of family."

"You're just saying that 'cause you love Mr. Rem and you want me to, too. But I won't. Not ever." And with that, Stan stormed from the room.

Samantha had vowed when Phillip left that nothing would ever come before her kids—not herself, not another relationship.

Was that what she was doing now?

Chapter Seven

Samantha was ignoring him.

Harry knew it. He'd called last night, after the Halloween party, but she hadn't answered.

He'd called today, as well. She hadn't been available then, either, according to Seton, followed by Shane.

Harry's mom had made a Sunday meal for them, and since he had her across the table, he figured this was as good a time as any to have it out with her. "So, Mom, when are you going to tell me what you said to Samantha?"

His mom wore her best innocent look. The same one she'd worn when he was five and asked if there really was a Santa. "I don't know what you're talking about, Harry, dear. Al, would you please pass me the butter?"

"No." Allen stood. "I think right now I'm going to excuse myself and take a long walk. We've never visited Erie before, but you've talked about it so often, that maybe it's time I make its acquaintance. So, you two sit here and talk. I'll be gone for a while."

Allen George walked to the front door of Harry's place. "A very long walk," he shouted back over his shoulder.

Harry had always liked Allen. He might have lived with his grandparents, but he'd spent time at the home his mother had built with Al, and Harry's two stepsisters, Karen and Barb. His stepfather had always gone out of his way to make Harry feel welcome.

"He's a good guy," Harry said to his mother.

"Yes, he is. Would you please pass me the butter?"

Harry slid the container over to his mom. "And it's nice that he left us to this discussion."

"What discussion is that, Harry dear?" She spread butter on her bread, studiously avoiding looking at him.

"Oh, Mom, whenever you use the word *dear,* I know you've done something. What now? What did you say to Samantha?"

His mother forgot about buttering her bread, and let the knife fall, butter-ladened, to the plate. "Now, Harry, I don't want you to be mad— I told her that neither of you are in a good place to start a relationship. You're coming home to Columbus in just about a month, and both you and Samantha are still getting over long-term relationships. The best this could be is a rebound relationship, and we all know how those end. I said as much to her." His mother picked up the knife and began spreading the butter on her bread, with all the care of someone painting a landscape.

"Mom," Harry said gently. He knew she meant well, but he was thirty-five, and able to handle his own affairs. "Mom, the first man you dated after you and Dad divorced was Al, and that seems to have held up well for a rebound relationship."

His mom got that warm glow to her face. "Allen and I are different."

"What if Samantha and I are different, too?"

"Sweetheart, I know you're still missing Teresa and Lucas. You can't replace them with some ready-made family, especially not one with issues. And this one has issues. I saw how that oldest boy, Seton, was glaring at you."

"Stan." He'd seen Stan shoot him more than one dark look, so he didn't bother to deny his mother's assessment. "Stan's the oldest. And he has had problems with the fact his mother and father divorced. Problems that were there before Samantha and I became friends."

"Problems that are exacerbated by your friendship— if that's what you insist on calling it—with his mother."

"Friendship," Harry reiterated.

"Honey, calling what's going on between you and Samantha a friendship is like calling the Superbowl a mere football game. I saw how you looked at her at the Halloween party and I mentioned it to her."

Harry wasn't about to admit it, but what he was feeling for Samantha did go beyond a friendship. He had been avoiding analyzing how far beyond. "Maybe there is something more between Samantha and me, but the truth is, Mom, whatever it is, it is between us, and you had no right—"

His mother was normally a mellow person, rarely given to fits of anger. But as her cheeks flushed and her eyes narrowed, Harry realized he'd said the wrong thing because she was more than a little annoyed.

"Don't you give me the you-have-no-right speech, Harris Paul Remington. I have every right. Every right in the world. I am your mother. Don't you think it kills me to see how much pain you've gone through by losing Teresa and Lucas? Don't you think I know the only reason you ever tried building a family with her was to replace the one you lost when your dad and I divorced?"

"Mom, that had nothing to do—"

She was too incensed to listen to him. "Lie to

yourself all you want to, but you can't lie to me. I know you've never forgiven me or your father for divorcing."

"Mom, nothing could be further from the truth. I might have been young, but I was old enough to know that you and Dad had been unhappy. Really unhappy. Just as I know you both found new relationships that were right. And I love you both enough to be glad of that."

"Then why wouldn't you move in with either of us?" There was no anger in her voice now. Only sadness and confusion. The rosy glow in her cheeks faded, as well. "I know it was years ago, but Harry, it killed me that you stayed with your grandparents. We both asked you to come with us. And both of us loved you enough to accept whatever parent you chose. But you stayed with my mom and dad, and just visited us. Just visited me. I missed you, Harry. I can't tell you how many nights I cried wanting you to be with me."

Hearing he'd made his mom cry bothered him. "Mom, it was years ago. I was young and confused. You built a new family with Al and the girls. I was part of your old family. I didn't feel as if I fit in."

"That's how you felt? As if I left both you and your father behind to build a new life for myself?"

Listening to her phrase it like that, he knew he'd been unfair. "Back then, I just couldn't figure out where I belonged."

"You belonged with me."

Hearing her say the words with such force and certainty made Harry realize how much his actions had hurt her.

"Mom, I never meant to hur—"

"It's okay, Harry," she interrupted. "I know you didn't mean to hurt me. You yourself were hurting. I should have forced you to move in with me. I should have fought to make you feel as if you belonged, even if the person I had to fight was you." She took his hand. "We can't change what happened. I might have caused you heartache then, but I can try to save you from some now. I'm willing to fight anyone, even you, to do that. That's why I spoke to Samantha, and I'm not going to apologize for interfering."

He sighed. "I'm not asking you to apologize. But I am asking you to let me live my own life."

"I did that when you were in high school, when I should have ordered you to move in with Al and me."

She'd never complained about his choice in all these years. Now, she couldn't seem to stop mentioning it. "Maybe you're right, Mom. Still, we ended up okay. I might not have felt as if I fit into your new family, but I always knew you loved me. Always."

She leaned over and kissed his cheek. "Thank you for that."

"And you're also right that Teresa and Lucas leaving tore at me. I don't know that the pain will ever truly go away. But it wasn't because I missed out on having another family, although that's part of it. I loved Teresa, although maybe not enough because I've recovered from that. However, there's no recovering from losing Lucas. I still love him. I miss him. That sort of pain doesn't stop."

"I know that. I understand that. But I don't want you rebounding and feeling even worse."

"Mom, there's no worry about rebounding. Samantha and I are…" He paused, trying to fill in the blank. "We're friends."

Friends. Yes, they were friends. They were notdating friends.

He'd thought that was enough, but with sudden clarity, he realized it wasn't.

Not-dating friends.

They were more than that.

He'd been working hard at not analyzing his feelings for Samantha. He had all kinds of excuses to avoid getting too close—the same excuses his mother had just used.

He was leaving to go back to Columbus. They were both just getting out of relationships. Her oldest didn't like him. They all sounded hollow now.

He needed time to sort it all out. Time to himself.

His mother didn't argue, but he could see that she didn't believe him. All she said was, "I love you, Harry."

"I love you, too. So, I hope you won't take it the wrong way when I ask, when are you and Al leaving for home?" He was teasing.

Well, mainly he was teasing.

He appreciated that she was concerned, but he needed to do things his own way.

"You shouldn't sound so enthusiastic," she said with a chuckle. "We're leaving as soon as Al comes back from his walk. I came, uninvited, because I'm worried about you. I want you home in Columbus."

"I'm fine, Mom. I'm just sorry that you're blaming yourself for all my problems. Teresa and my failed relationship… That's on us. It's not your fault. Not Dad's fault. I wanted more than Teresa was able to give. I'd known that for a long time, but just couldn't admit it to myself."

"And Samantha?" his mother asked gently.

"I'm not sure where we stand, but whatever happens, it's not your fault, either. I'm an adult."

"Harry, you'll always be my son. I'll try to not worry so much, if you'll promise to spend Thanksgiving with us."

"I'll be in Erie over Thanksgiving. How about if I promise to spend some time with you at Christmas?"

"Good enough." She kissed his cheek again. "I do love you. No matter what happened between your father and I, the two of us always have and always will."

Harry felt lighter than he had in years as he spent a while just talking to his mom. He waved goodbye to her and Al, and she called out assurances she'd see him soon. Part of him groaned at the thought, another part was pleased.

Listening to her, he realized that he'd hurt her by not moving in with her and becoming a part of her new family. To hurt her had never been his intent. He'd been young, confused and maybe just a little angry that he didn't have the "perfect family."

He'd loved Teresa. He didn't like his mother's accusation that he'd only used her and Lucas as a ready-made family. He'd fallen for Teresa long before he came to know and care for her son. Seven years they'd been together as a family. He'd even felt parental.

So, although Harry wasn't sure about much, he was positive he wasn't looking for another ready-made family. He wasn't stupid enough to want to go through the pain of losing a third family. So he was sure he wasn't using Samantha for that.

To be honest, the last thing he wanted was to date a woman with kids.

They were friends.

He cared about her.

More and more, to be honest.

They'd set ground rules to their friendship, and he'd planned to abide by them, but he really wanted something deeper. There were three problems that stood in the path of that.

One, he wasn't sure she did. Samantha seemed totally satisfied with their relationship on a totally platonic level.

Two, he was leaving Erie in a few weeks.

And finally, number three—Samantha had kids. And one of them, Stan, didn't care for Harry. The boy had made that abundantly clear.

That was a lot to overcome in a month.

Harry felt more confused than ever.

He tried calling Samantha again. This time he got her answering machine.

She was probably upset about his mom. He'd have to find a way to make it up to her.

TUESDAY MORNINGS SAMANTHA usually had off, but today, she was free all day since Dr. Jackson was teaching a class and not seeing patients. Rather than doing her grocery shopping or picking up her dry cleaning, Samantha found herself once again walking down the hall of Erie Elementary towards the principal's office.

She'd avoided Harry's calls Sunday, and had skipped out on the monthly PTA meeting last night. After all, what were they going to do to her? They'd already put her on the Social Planning Committee.

So, she called Michelle, gave her apologies and a lame excuse about a headache and spent the night at home waiting for the phone to ring, even as she dreaded it.

It hadn't rung.

No, it had caught her this morning as she prepared for a mile-long list of errands.

It wasn't that she didn't want to talk to Harry, she simply didn't know what to say to him. That's what it all came down to. Harry's mother's comments had knocked her legs out from under her, and she didn't know how to get back up.

It hadn't been Harry on the phone. It had been the school secretary. And she'd had pure business in her tone as she said, "Mrs. Williams, you need to come in. It's about an incident."

"I'll be right there," Samantha had promised.

When she walked into the office, Mrs. Vioni didn't smile a greeting. She merely nodded toward the principal's door and said, "They're waiting for you."

They're.

Not just Harry. Harry and one of her kids.

Or maybe more.

Maybe all three boys?

Samantha suppressed a groan as she knocked on the office door.

Harry called, "Come in."

Harry was behind his desk looking stern, and Stan sat in a chair across from him, looking belligerent. But underneath the tough-guy facade, Samantha saw confusion and nervousness.

This was not going to be good.

"Mom," Stan began, but Samantha gave him a look—a mom-look that had taken her years to perfect—and he snapped his mouth shut.

She took the empty chair next to her son and asked Harry, "So, what happened this time?"

"Stan was caught writing graffiti in the restroom, he—"

Samantha swung around so she was facing Stan, who was studiously staring at his knees. "Stan." Her voice sharp to her own ears. He looked up slowly, a deer-in-the-headlights look in his eyes. She purposefully forced herself to speak calmly and slowly. "I thought after last year's incident, we were done with that kind of thing?"

"Mom, I—"

"I don't want excuses, and I don't want to hear any more from your principal. I want you to pony up and tell me why we're here again, and more importantly tell me why. You know defacing someone else's property isn't permitted. So explain it to me."

Stan jumped out of his chair, as if he couldn't remain seated another moment as his anger bubbled over. Samantha could see him working to get the words out, forcing them past that fury. "He—" Stan gave an angry jerk in Harry's direction "—comes into our lives and thinks he can play dad." He lowered his voice and said, *"Here, kids, I'll put up a swing for you. I'll play with you. I'll take you out for pizza, or come to Sunday dinner."*

Stan took a deep breath, but there was no calmness in his voice as he continued. "Well, I have a dad, I don't need him, and you don't need him. Nobody needs him. I guess that's why his girlfriend left and took that other boy with her, 'cause they didn't need him, either."

Samantha winced at the ugliness in Stan's words and she turned to look at Harry, who had visibly paled. She knew Stan had hit his mark.

"Stanford Robert Williams, apologize to Mr. Remington for those hateful, hurtful words."

For a moment she didn't think he was going to obey, but he muttered, "Sorry," though he didn't look in Harry's direction.

"Sit back down and pay attention to me." She waited as slowly he sat back in the chair. "Stan, we've been over this and over this."

"I know that. But he…" He jerked his head in Harry's direction again. "He doesn't. I was walking through the hall today and he says, *'Hey, Stan, tell your mom to call me tonight, okay?'* Like I'm his answering machine, or something. He said it in front of all my friends. They all started talking about you, about how you were dating the principal. I told 'em you weren't and Marcus kept at it. I wanted to punch him, but I didn't. But when I went into the bathroom, no one was there, and I wrote *Principal Remington sucks* on the wall. I'm not sure why. I didn't mean to. It just happened."

Samantha had heard the it-just-happened excuse before, and had frequently called it into question; however, seeing the frustration and anger on Stan's face, she understood. "Stan, I can believe that having your friends all tease you—"

"They were singing that stupid kids' rhyme about you and Mr. Remington sitting in a tree."

She reached over and put her hand on his shoulder, sensing he needed the contact. "Stan, that's got to be embarrassing, and I'm so sorry it happened. Yet I still can't condone graffiti. You promised after last year that it wouldn't happen again."

"I know, and I'm sorry."

"Why don't you excuse Mr. Remington and I while we discuss your punishment, but be assured at the very least you'll be staying after and cleaning off or painting over that graffiti." She turned to Harry. "Is that all right with you?"

"Yes. Why don't you return to class, Stan, and report here before lunch."

Stan glared at Harry and said, "Fine," before stomping toward the door.

"And, Stan," Harry called, stopping him in his tracks. "I'm sorry I embarrassed you in front of your friends. That wasn't my intent."

Stan didn't respond. He simply continued out the door, slamming it behind him.

"Samantha, I'm sorry."

He'd found some of his color, but she could tell that he was still smarting from Stan's outburst.

"Me, too, Harry. He must have overheard something we said…."

Harry waved his hand. "It doesn't matter."

But it did matter.

"What else do you think you need to do to him, in addition to having him remove the graffiti?"

"I think that will be sufficient. It sounds like he's already had quite a time of it with his friends because of me."

"Because of us. Stan's having more problems with our—" she hesitated "—our friendship than I imagined. He came to me again this weekend, and sounded so much like a little boy as he told me he wanted me and his dad to get back together. I told him that as much as Phillip and I both loved him—love all the kids—it wasn't going to happen. I'm afraid today's incident has something to do with that conversation."

"And of course, my huge blunder didn't help. I'm sorry. And I'm sorry about my mother. I tried calling—"

"My first instinct is to tell you that I was busy with the kids yesterday, especially Stan. Frankly, there's also what your mom said. It was comfortable having you around, thinking of you as a friend, but Harry, I'm sure that right now isn't the time for anything more than that. I know that's all we are, but if other people are seeing it as something more than it is? And given that Stan's going through something, maybe it's better if we saw a little less of each other. After all, you're leaving soon."

"Geri just called today and says she has a hot prospect she's interviewing for the principal's job, so I might finish at Erie Elementary sooner than I thought. I'd promised Geri I'd stay until my classes finished in December. I've got to get back to my job in Columbus the second week in December."

She wanted to ask, "That soon?" But she didn't. "Do you miss it? Miss your friends and family?"

"Sometimes. I miss my Saturday morning basketball league with a group of teachers from school. I miss my mother dropping in and basically making me crazy. I miss the kids I worked with there. But so much of my life there was tied up with Teresa and Lucas…" He shrugged. "Well, you know how it is."

Samantha did. She used to be part of a couple, and so many of the things she did were as part of that twosome. Learning to do things solo, to build a life on her own was hard. But having Michelle and Carly in her corner was helping. So was having Harry. She didn't want to lose that. She wanted to be sure he understood that. "Yes, I know how it is. And I'm glad you're here in Erie. Glad you and I reconnected. And, Harry, we'll still be friends, but I have to put the kids—Stan—first."

"Samantha, I wanted to talk to you about that. You see, my mother might not be wrong. I don't think our not-dating dates are working because I think, maybe it's more than friendship on my end."

"It can't be." Samantha stood, wanting—no, needing—to get out of the room. Despite her urge, she held her ground. "We can't let it be. Either of us. We're neither of us ready for anything more."

Rather than respond, Harry got up, as well, and walked around the desk. He took her into his arms, and gently—oh, so tenderly—kissed her. It was a soft kiss of introduction. Tentative, growing bolder and more decisive with every second—or was it every minute?—that it went on.

A small voice in Samantha's head said, *Pull away. Stop this now.*

She didn't listen as she took control of the kiss, deepening it as she pressed herself into Harry's chest. She needed to be closer.

When they finally broke apart, Samantha took an immediate step back, wanting to put some distance between them as much as she'd wanted to be closer a moment ago.

"I think we have to admit what we've been developing over the last few weeks runs deeper than just friendship." Harry's voice sounded rather raspy. "There's friendship there, but there's more, Sami. At least there is for me."

He waited, watching her.

Samantha didn't know what to say. "Harry, you're not listening. Stan's very troubled by our being friends. What would happen to him if whatever we have is more than that?"

"What about you, Sami?" It was the second time he'd used her old nickname. "What about how you feel?"

"Maybe there's more than friendship for me, too. After that kiss—" which still had her feeling rather breathless "—I'd be a fool to deny it. And I'd want to explore my feelings further, if there weren't so many strikes against us. I don't want to be a short-term, rebound relationship for you. And I don't think that's what you want for me."

"Samantha, what we're feeling is special."

"And I'd take a chance on it if it were just me, just us. But I can't risk my kids. They're confused enough already. That's evident in Stan's graffiti."

"He'd adjust," Harry insisted.

"You won't be here long enough for that to happen. And even if you were, we couldn't be sure he'd ever come to terms with us being in a relationship. From what you've said, you never managed it with your stepfather."

"I did." There wasn't much heat in Harry's protest.

"Liar," Samantha said gently. "You told me yourself that both of your parents wanted you to live with them. They felt you were old enough to decide, and rather than choosing one of them you stayed with your grandparents."

"Because I didn't want to start another new school."

Samantha gave Harry a look that he could be dishonest with himself, but she knew better. "Because you were afraid you wouldn't fit into either of your parents' new families. I don't want that for my son."

"Even if it means sacrificing your own happiness?"

"Even then." She took a step, closing the distance she'd placed between them, and kissed his cheek. "Harry, I'd rather let you go now when it's all so new and, if you're honest, undefined. I'd rather call our friendship quits now, when we're not sure what, if anything more, we could become."

"It will hurt, Samantha."

"Yes, it will. But like a bandage, it's better to rip it off now and get it over with."

"You're sure?"

She hesitated. She wasn't sure. Wasn't sure at all, but she nodded. "Yes, it's for the best. You'll be keeping Stan after school?" she asked, all business.

"Yes."

"Then, I'll…" She started to say, *I'll talk to you soon,* but she wouldn't. She was cutting off everything but their school ties, and they both knew it. So she settled for, "I'll see you around."

He nodded.

She felt his eyes on her as she walked through the door. She shut it behind her as quickly as possible. She was doing the right thing. The only sane and sensible thing.

She was sure.

At least, she was mostly sure.

THE REST OF THE DAY was a haze of keeping busy. Samantha ran her errands, then hit the kitchen and baked. She didn't bother sucking in her stomach, or looking for a silver lining as she made chocolate chip cookies, a chocolate cake and even put a loaf of bread out to rise. She started a stew and put it in the oven, as well.

She was going to throw that stupid book out.

She still had more than an hour before the kids would be home, so she cleaned the house, top to bottom, retrieving Legos, action figures and Barbies from under the couch, and a small catnip ball that Grunge had disdained and buried between the cushions.

Relieved when she glanced at the clock and saw the kids would be home at any minute. They often walked the six blocks on nice days, and today was a beautiful day. Cold enough to remind everyone in Erie that winter was on the horizon.

She put away the vacuum, and was waiting in the foyer as the younger three kids ran across the porch and flung open the door.

"Mom, Stan had to stay after," Seton screamed, by way of greeting.

"Yes, I know. He won't be long."

"What'd he do now?" Shane asked, throwing his coat and bookbag into the corner, and kicking off his shoes with such precise aim they landed on top of them. "Carrie said he was playing with matches."

"No. No matches."

Seton asked, "So what *did* he do?" He had a particular gleam of big-brother-idol-worship in his eye.

"Let's not worry about Stan. Stella, how was your day?"

Stella had come in quietly and shut the door. She'd then taken off her shoes and lined them neatly on the mat against the wall. At her mother's question, she opened her bookbag and retrieved her take-home folder. "We had a lady come in and talk about all the dogs that need homes. And Mom, you said you'd think about us gettin' a dog. We have a big house and a dog would fit in really good."

"Oh, honey." Samantha had said she'd think about a dog, but now she wasn't sure if she could cope with one more thing without collapsing.

"Come on, Mom. They're having an open house tonight from the Human S'ciety—"

"Humane Society," Shane corrected her.

"Yeah, them," Stella agreed. "They're open late. We could go look, at least."

"Yeah. Come on, Mom," her brothers chorused. "We'd just look."

"Please?" all three said in unison.

Samantha melted. "I'll think about it. But first, homework."

She meant to think…and say no. Although after a very sullen Stan came home and did his homework without complaint, then ate quietly as the other three continued their just-visit-the-shelter campaign, Samantha caught Stan looking up with something akin to hope in his eyes. So she found herself saying, "Okay." The kids got up and ran out of the dining room—she presumed to get ready to go. "Just to look," she called after them.

"Are you all right?" she asked Stan. "You didn't say much at dinner."

"I'm sorry about today," he repeated. "I apologized to Mr. Remington again, too."

"I guess that's all I can ask for. Everyone makes

mistakes, Stan. You've fixed it and apologized. We're good. Now come on, we're visiting that shelter."

He smiled then, the smallest upturn of his lips, but Samantha felt a bit lighter because of it.

They all piled into the van and headed to the Humane Society, the dinner dishes still unwashed in the sink.

"Mommy, I bet there'll be tons of kids from school here," Stella chirped merrily.

But there was only one other car in the parking lot when they arrived. Samantha felt as if she had the word *sucker* tattooed on her forehead.

"Now remember, we're just looking," Samantha warned. Not that anyone was listening. The kids were already out of the car and heading into the building.

Samantha followed the kids, who'd started through the pens of animals. Her heart always broke a little as she looked at the faces of the animals who were dejected and barely noticed as they passed. Some wagged their tails hopefully; some played coy, shooting well-timed looks at the kids.

This was a mistake. Samantha knew it the minute she reached the end of an aisle and found all four kids standing in front of a cage.

"Mommy," was all Stella said.

Samantha was pretty sure why this dog was relegated to the back. It seemed defeated, as if it knew that no one was going to adopt anything as odd-looking as it was.

Okay, *odd* was a generous word.

Ugly was more accurate.

If an old English mastiff, with its big droopy eyes and jowls, along with a copious drooling problem, mated with a kinky-haired poodle, this dog would be their child. The dog had tight black and brown curls all over its body, including its wobbly jowls. One eye was ringed, as if a bull's-eye marked the depressed dog.

Add to that it was ninety pounds at least. Obviously, its depression hadn't damaged its appetite.

"That's the one, Mom," Stella hollered. "That's our dog. Her name is Marmalade. Grunge is going to love her. And she'll love Grunge."

Samantha doubted the validity of the statements. Grunge didn't like anyone, particularly a hundredish-pound dog. She said, "Kids, we were only looking. Remember?" Still, she knew it was hopeless as all four sets of eyes turned to her with the same longing the dog had.

"She's big enough that we won't hurt her if we trip on her," Seton said.

"And she doesn't look like we could scare her," Shane assured her.

To be honest, the dog appeared as if she was so low that nothing, not even Samantha's brood, could put her off.

"Could we visit with her?" Shane asked. "They've got a visiting room."

Samantha meant to say no.

She meant to say, "We're not getting a dog."

She meant to remind them again that the cat would not be happy.

Which is why it was a mystery when the word *yes* flashed in her mind instead.

The Society volunteer who'd settled them in the visiting room, then brought Marmalade, said, "What she lacks in physical beauty, she makes up for with a spar-kling personality. I've hated that no one's even taken a second look at her."

Samantha watched her kids give the dog a second, then a third look. Stella hugged the monster, while the boys petted her, and talked excitedly about how they'd take her for walks.

Marmalade tried to maintain her depression. The dog made a valiant effort to remain aloof. Yet the kids didn't seem to notice and gradually, Marmalade warmed to them, her long tail started to wag, slowly at first, then faster and faster. Her huge tongue started to loll out the side of her mouth as she gave the kids a big dog grin. Then, she gave up and dropped all pretense of keeping her distance, and started licking whatever child was closest.

"Gross," they all hollered, but their faces were masks of delight. Even Stan's.

"Mom," Shane said. "She's a really nice dog." He didn't ask, but she could see the question in his eyes. He'd fallen in love. Head-over-heels, hopelessly in love with the dog.

"Can we keep her?" Stella asked in a small voice. "I've got twelve dollars at home to help pay."

"I've got fifteen," Shane added.

Pretty soon they were all discussing what money they had available, and how much Marmalade and all her doggie requirements might cost them.

"If it's not enough," Stan said as he turned to her, obviously ready to make a deal. "Mom, you can keep our allowances until we pay it off. If we can get her." There was a look in his eyes that said he wanted the dog every bit as much as his siblings, but he didn't think she'd agree.

Four sets of eyes pleaded.

As if knowing her fate was being decided, Marmalade walked over to Samantha, sniffed her once, then sat down with a thud and stared at her.

Samantha didn't bother to quibble. She didn't try to extract promises that the kids would walk the dog or scoop up dog poop. And looking at Marmalade, there was bound to be dog poop.

Samantha smiled at her kids, and simply said, "Yes."

It was one of those perfect mom moments. The kids were bouncing out of their skins with excitement. And Marmalade bounced right along with them, which was a sight to behold.

As Samantha filled in all the forms, and watched the kids play with the dog, she wished she had the power to make them that happy every day. She listened to their laughter and knew this should be enough. Knowing her kids were happy had to be enough.

She glanced at Stan, who hadn't done much smiling lately. He was grinning, exactly like his siblings.

He caught her looking at him and smiled back at her.

Yes, she'd make this enough.

Maybe someday the kids would be ready to allow a new man into their lives, but they weren't now, or at least Stan wasn't.

She thought about Harry leaving in a few weeks. She did the math in her head. Just thirty-three days.

Maybe it would be easier when he did move and was totally out of reach.

Maybe.

But she doubted it.

Chapter Eight

Friday couldn't come soon enough for Samantha. She had all four kids in the car, which she parked a block from Erie Elementary. She'd agreed to bring them to the basketball game only after they promised to watch Stella.

"Now, if there are any problems, I'll hear about it," Samantha warned as they entered the noisy gym. Immediately, she spotted Heidi selling snacks at the PTA table.

"Hi, Heidi."

"Hey, Samantha. Are you here to work the table?" There was hope in her eyes.

"Sorry," she apologized. "I'd love to, but I'm on my way to the committee meeting for the Thanksgiving Pageant."

"How's that going?" Heidi asked as she took two quarters from second-grader Izzy Rizzo in exchange for a chocolate bar.

Heidi was one of those wonder-moms who did absolutely everything. Normally, nothing seemed to phase her, but tonight, at the snack stand, she looked worn out and frazzled.

"Everything's fine," Samantha assured her, even though it was a huge lie. "Is everything okay with you?"

Heidi hesitated.

"Heidi?" Samantha asked. She and Heidi were friendly. Not as close as Heidi was with Michelle, but they'd chatted now and again at school functions. "If you need something…" She left the sentence hanging.

Samantha thought Heidi was going to open up about something, but then the PTA president shook her head. "No, I'm fine."

"Okay. If you change—"

Heidi interrupted her. "You worry about the committee. That's a huge weight off of my shoulders. I'll get the rest."

Samantha nodded. "Anyway, I'll be just down the hall."

"No problem. I'll keep an eye on the kids."

Feeling better, she focused on how anxious she was to unload on Michelle and Carly. As she walked she could just imagine them poor-babying her over Harry. She could almost hear them as they tripped over one another trying to comfort her.

After discussing Harry at length, Samantha would turn to her actual PTA news, and she'd drop her bombshell. Michelle and Carly would both, once again, commiserate, and both, of course, offer assistance to pull the Thanksgiving Pageant together.

And Samantha was sure she would need all the help she could get.

It had all seemed so simple at that first PTA meeting.

A Thanksgiving Pageant with a teacher who'd done that kind of thing dozens of times. Samantha had even sat through three of Mrs. Tarbot's third-grade pageants starring Stan, Seton and Shane. She knew how competent and organized the woman was. How could she have suspected then what a fiasco this would turn into?

At first, all seemed well. Mrs. Tarbot was running rehearsals, and had most of the costumes at hand. Samantha had promised to show up at a few of the rehearsals so she'd know the play and could prompt the kids who forgot their lines on the day of the performance. And she'd said she'd come in a couple mornings to help fit last year's costumes to this year's class. Stella was beside herself with excitement, anxious to hear what role she'd landed.

Yes, everything was going well.

Then...

No, she wasn't going to think about it now, she would wait and tell Michelle and Carly and be soothed by their comfort.

She almost sprinted into the meeting room with a box of chocolate-covered strawberries and wept with relief to see that Michelle and Carly were both at the table already.

"You'll never guess what happened this week," she said without preamble as she set down the strawberries and took off her coat.

"That's what I said when I came in." Carly sounded depressed.

"Me, too," Michelle echoed, sounding agitated, which was totally at odds with her normally placid demeanor. "We waited for you before we started spilling."

"You guys start, then I'll tell you my news." Samantha took a strawberry to soothe her own anxiousness as she waited.

Carly took one, as well. "Michelle first."

"It's Brandon," Michelle blurted. "He wants to find his father."

Samantha knew that Michelle was raising her nephew, who was in Seton's class. She'd assumed the boy's father had passed away along with Michelle's sister. But obviously, that wasn't the case.

"You don't know where his father is?" Carly asked.

"I don't know *who* his father is, much less where he is. That's the problem. What if I help Brandon find the man, and he's—" she hesitated "—he's not the kind of man you'd want in a young boy's life? I met some of my sister Tara's boyfriends, and believe me, there's a very good possibility that's the case. What if we find him and he hurts Brandon? Not physically. I'd never let that happen. But what if he tells him he doesn't want him? Or what if…" Her voice dropped to hardly more than a whisper. "What if he does want him and…full custody?"

"Oh, Michelle." Samantha patted her friend's hand.

"Brandon came to live with me right after I graduated college. I'm embarrassed to admit that part of me hoped someone else would claim him. My mom. His father. I was young and didn't know the first thing about raising a boy. Now, he's my life. My sister made a lot of mistakes, and I couldn't do anything to stop her. But Brandon was her greatest achievement and she trusted him to me. How could I possibly let him go? He needs me. And I need him. Maybe that's selfish, but I don't know who I'd be if I wasn't Brandon's aunt. "

Carly leaned over and hugged Michelle. "No matter what happens, you'll always be his aunt. He'll always love you."

"How can I take that risk? How can I help him find someone neither of us knows, when there's the chance that I'll lose Brandon to him?"

Samantha understood completely, but she also knew seventh-grade boys, and wasn't sure Brandon would accept a flat-out no from his aunt as an answer. "What did you tell him?"

"I told him we'd wait. When he's eighteen I'll do everything in my power to help him find his father."

"How'd he take that?" Carly asked.

"He was furious. He's still hardly talking to me. And Bran and I don't fight like that. I don't know how to handle it…to handle him."

Samantha ached for Michelle. Even though Phillip hadn't seen much of the kids right after their divorce, he was back now and steadier than he'd been in years. She knew that having him in the kids' lives was good for all of them.

Yet she could understand Michelle's concern that Brandon's father might not be such a positive influence. "He knows you love him and he'll come around," she promised. "We've had our own hurdles at my house, but the kids know I love them, and that's why they always get over being mad. So will Brandon."

"I hope so." Michelle didn't sound so sure. "I hope our talk was the end of it. I just hate having him angry at me, and feeling as if I've somehow let him down."

Both Carly and Samantha comforted Michelle until it was obvious that she was feeling better.

"Thanks, guys." She turned to Carly. "Your turn."

"Dean and I had another meeting with a mediator, trying to finish the divorce settlement. As soon as that's worked out, it's all done. My marriage is over." She paused. "No, I take that back, the marriage was over the moment I caught him with his secretary on my couch. I just want this settled before Thanksgiving. The divorce was in January, despite the fact we hadn't divided the marital assets. I graduate in December, and I'd really like to go into the new year with a degree, a new job and a totally completed divorce. I can't spare much more time for this. I've got a couple huge papers due, on top of getting ready for the start of the holiday season."

Samantha and Michelle both offered support as Carly continued to talk about her ex, and how he'd balked about paying for her to go back to school, despite the fact she'd quit college to put him through law school.

As Carly wound down, Samantha had a sinking feeling in the pit of her stomach as she realized how busy her friends' lives were. Neither of them had time to help with the Thanksgiving Pageant. She'd imagined them consoling her, and jumping to her aid when she told them that Mrs. Tarbot had appendicitis. It had only happened today, and she was pretty sure the word hadn't spread on the Erie Elementary grapevine yet. Mrs. Tarbot was going to be out for a while, and wouldn't be able to oversee the Thanksgiving Pageant. Samantha had spoken to the sub, a Ms. Hahn, who had a four-month-old baby at home and went on and on about getting home as soon as school was out. There was no way she was going to stay after and help. Which meant Samantha would be directing the pageant, and fitting the costumes and preparing the set.

How hard could it be? So, she didn't mention Mrs. Tarbot. Or Ms. Hahn.

She'd deal with the pageant on her own, somehow.

Still, she needed comforting. So as Michelle and Carly looked at her, signaling it was her turn, she said, "I broke off my friendship with Harry."

The words tumbled one over another as she told them everything. About Harry's mom, about Stan, about the kiss. "So, I ended it. I'm sure it's for the best. He's leaving soon anyways."

"But you didn't want to." The gentleness in Michelle's voice almost undid her.

She replayed the kiss in her mind, and caught her fingers moving toward her lips, as if she could recapture it. She firmly brought her hand back to the table, and nodded. "No, I didn't want to, but right now, the kids have to come first. Stan has to come first."

They continued to talk, sharing, unburdening, reassuring. Again, Samantha didn't mention Mrs. Tarbot, not even when Michelle asked, "We're supposed to be here to talk about the Thanksgiving Pageant. Is there anything we can do?"

Samantha forced a smile and lied through her teeth, "No, there's nothing either of you need to worry about. I've got it under control."

Samantha knew she was right not to tell her friends about her predicament. Now, if only she could figure out how to handle all the pageant details on her own.

HARRY KNEW THE PTA SOCIAL committee moms met every other Friday, and that this was their week. He tried to ignore the light from the meeting room as he walked along the hallway. Every part of him wanted to wait and talk to Samantha, instead, he forced himself to turn left and head into the gym. He might be only an interim principal, but while he was here, he'd do his best, and that meant coming to as many school functions as humanly possible. He figured he'd be able to catch a bit more than the last half of the game.

The gym was full. Erie Elementary was a tight-knit community, and the school families turned out in droves for any event. He was greeted by a number of people as he made his way into the gym. He glanced at the scoreboard. Home 10, Visitors 3.

"Hi, Mr. Remington," Heidi called out from the snack table.

"Harry, Heidi." He made his way over to her. "You can call me Harry," he reminded her.

She smiled ruefully. "I don't want to seem too informal in front of the kids."

"I doubt any of them would notice over the din. The game seems to be going well."

"It's always going well if we're winning," she said with a smile that didn't quite reach her eyes.

"Is everything okay?" he asked.

"You're the second person to ask me that today. I must look a fright." She patted at her hair.

"That's not it. You just seem…not quite yourself." Granted, he didn't know the woman personally, but he'd had numerous meetings with her since starting at Erie Elementary, and she definitely wasn't her normal chipper self. He couldn't quite put his finger on it, but something was off.

"I'm fine," she said. "And you?"

"I'm fine, too," he assured her, knowing even as he said the words they were both liars. "If you need anything…"

She nodded. "I won't, but it's kind of you." She smiled. "You better go mingle with the school families and watch some of the game. I wouldn't want to make Samantha jealous." She grinned, obviously teasing.

"What?"

She looked stricken. "Oh, Mr. Remington, I didn't mean. I mean, I did. I was only kidding. I mean we, all saw the two of you at the Halloween party and assumed… I mean—"

"That's an awful lot of 'I means' for one sentence. And it's okay, you just caught me by surprise. Samantha and I are, well, we're friends. We knew each other as kids, and she's been kind to me since I don't really have any old contacts in town. That's all."

Heidi didn't need to know that Samantha was more than a kind old friend who'd taken him under her wing. He thought back to the kiss. A lot more.

"I see. I'll be sure to spread the word and stop various tongues from wagging."

"I'd appreciate that." He made his way into the crowd milling around one end of the bleachers. He nodded and made all the appropriate greetings, but his heart wasn't in it. It wasn't in the game, either, though he clapped as the home team pulled even further ahead.

He thought about Samantha in the meeting room. Maybe he should go check on her.

"Mr. Rem," came a small voice.

He looked down and saw Stella standing there grinning at him. He knelt down so he was closer at her eye-level. "Hey, Stell. How're things?"

"I lost the boys. They're supposed to be watching me, but they told me to stay in my seat, and I don't know where they are."

"Would you like me to help you find them?"

She nodded, her brown braids bouncing against her shoulders. She looked at him then, her eyes, so like Samantha's, trusting.

"Come on. We'll find them."

It wasn't hard to locate Seton. He was dangling from the ledge of the top bleacher. And after a stern warning that the boys take better care of their sister, Harry went back to his mingling and tried to forget Samantha was nearby.

He kept trying to forget throughout the rest of the game. When Samantha came for her kids, he spotted her and waved. She gave a small wave back, gathered Stella and the boys and started out the door, but not before turning and giving him another look.

He waved again, and she nodded, then ushered the kids out.

Leaving Harry wishing he was going with them.

THAT SUNDAY EVENING, Samantha decided there was such a thing as a silver lining.

The fact that she was so busy doing everything for the pageant meant she didn't have time to fret about Harry. At least that's what she told herself. But for someone who wasn't spending a lot of time thinking about Harry, she was spending a lot of time thinking about how she was not thinking about him.

He'd looked sad as he'd waved at her from across the gym Friday night.

Samantha forced herself to glance up at the kids, who were playing their new game—tag Marmalade. She hadn't caught on to all the rules, but it seemed to center on a lot of running, shrieking and general pandemonium.

She clipped the thread. She was reattaching feathers to the turkey costume. She wasn't sure just what had happened at last year's pageant, but it obviously involved defeathering the turkey. There were exactly three feathers on the costume when she'd started. After an hour of sewing, there were maybe twenty. She glanced at the box and refused to think about how many more she had to go.

Grunge, who considered it beneath his dignity to play the game with the kids and the dog, leaped onto the couch and started batting the thread as she tried to get it through the eye of the needle.

"Grunge," she warned, but when the cat continued

batting the thread as if he hadn't heard her, she gave up and held the thread in place and let Grunge have at it as the dog and kids darted around the room.

If Harry were here, he'd be right in the thick of it, running and acting like a ten-year-old.

This had to stop. She had to stop thinking about Harry.

She pulled the thread away from Grunge, and picked up the needle, only to jab herself in the finger. "Ow."

The three younger kids didn't pay any attention to her but Stan stopped cold in his tracks. "You okay, Mom?"

"I just pricked my finger. You know that sewing isn't my forte, which is why my motto is—"

"If there's a hole, don't come to me," he finished for her.

She nodded. "I don't sew or iron." She hated ironing more than sewing, and that was saying something.

"So, why are you sewing on turkey feathers?" He came closer, standing near the edge of the couch, watching her intently.

"Sometimes you have to think of other people. The third-graders need the costumes for their pageant, so I'm sewing."

He frowned. "Why don't the other two moms help. They're supposed to, right?"

Both Michelle and Carly had heard about Mrs. Tarbot and called. Samantha had lied through her teeth, telling them that she and the sub had everything under control. She would need them the day of the pageant to help. Yes, she could have asked some of the other PTA parents for help, but that would have gotten back to Michelle and Carly, making them feel guilty.

No, this was an instance of it was easier to just do it herself. She was hoping she'd be so busy she'd forget about missing Harry.

"I can handle this."

"I could help then," he offered.

"Sewing? I mean, Stan, you know I try not to be sexist, if you want to sew, I'm all for it." She smiled and he laughed, which had been her intent.

"Well, not that, but I could help with the stage stuff. Me, Seton and Shane are pretty good with paint. Mr. Rem said—" He hesitated, as if not sure he should mention Harry.

"Yes…?" Samantha prompted, trying to give him her best talking-about-Harry-doesn't-bother-me look, though it did. Because talking about him meant she was thinking about him and that hurt.

"He said we did a good job on his office." He flopped onto the couch next to her, watching for her reaction.

"Yes, he did," she agreed. "He told me how great you all were getting his office painted."

"I don't know why he bothered with it. I mean, it's not like he's staying. He's temporary. That head-lady was in school on Friday showing some new guy around. Someone said he was going to be the new principal. That means Mr. Rem will be going back to Ohio soon." He punched at a pillow, presumably to make it more comfortable, but he used far more force than was needed.

Samantha could sense this wasn't just turkey feathers and painting scenery. "Maybe he felt better with his office set up. Sometimes you can't worry so much about what's coming up in the future that you miss out on what's happening right now."

"Well, right now, maybe you need some help with the stage stuff?"

She nodded. "Thanks for noticing. I will definitely take you up on your offer because the truth is I do need all the help I can get. Why don't I come to school tomorrow and we'll all stay after and work on it?"

"I'll help watch the little kids so they don't make things harder," he offered.

She smiled. "I appreciate that, honey."

Stan got off the couch, and returned to the tag game with his siblings and the dog, but he kept checking on her. Samantha couldn't quite read what was going on in his head, but she knew eventually he'd open up to her.

It was only a matter of time.

She thought about a new principal touring the school, then pushed it aside. She'd known Harry was going back to Columbus.

That was only a matter of time, as well.

THE WEEKEND WAS LESS than stellar. Harry went through the motions. He pretended to do his classwork. He pretended to do Erie Elementary work in case he had to hand things off to the new principal. But then Geri called and said the candidate she was grooming for the position had taken another offer. So he'd be heading back to the school next week.

The highlight of his weekend was a two-hour talk with Lucas Sunday evening. They'd discussed the ins and outs of Lucas's football season. "I'll send a tape, 'kay, Harry?"

"I can't wait, Lucas."

"Harry, can I come see you?"

That one innocent question broke Harry's heart. Lucas was Shane's age, and nowhere near old enough to travel on his own. "Well, L., I can't promise anything other than I'll see you as soon as it's possible. I miss you."

"Miss you, too, Harry. Lots. 'Night."

"'Night, bud."

Harry had fallen into a funk after that, not noticing that the house had long since gone dark until the phone rang. Everything in him wanted to pick up the receiver and hear Samantha's voice. Instead, it was his mom calling just to check on him.

She casually asked about Samantha, and when he said they'd decided not to see so much of each other she suggested, "That's probably for the best."

That's what he tried to tell himself as he went to bed, but he was finding it hard to believe. The truth of the matter was, he missed Samantha. Missed her far more than he should.

It was a relief to be at school on Monday. He didn't have to pretend to be busy, as Monday mornings were habitually packed with things that required his attention.

It was well after lunch when Harry looked up to find Stan standing in his doorway. The boy's expression was unreadable.

"Hi, Stan. Come on in."

The boy stepped into his office, and shut the door behind him. "Mrs. Vioni said I could come in 'cause, Mr. Remington, I need to talk to you."

"Have a seat, Stan." Harry waved at the chair.

Stan shuffled across the room, not looking happy to be in the office, but beneath the uneasiness was a sense of determination.

Harry put down his pen and simply waited as Stan took the seat and fidgeted for a few moments. Finally, the boy began, "I… Mrs. Tarbot's sick."

"Yes, I know. I've arranged a substitute for at least a few weeks. Is there a problem with Stella and the sub? Is she upset about Mrs. Tarbot?"

"Nah. She misses her, but she said Ms. Hahn is nice."

"I'm glad." Harry noted that Stan seemed to be struggling over what to say next.

"I…uh…" Stan hemmed and hawed. Suddenly in a

rush, he asked, "You know about the Thanksgiving Pageant?"

"Yes." Harry glanced at his desk calendar. "It's two weeks from tomorrow."

"Yeah, and my mom's doing everything on her own now 'cause Mrs. Tarbot's out sick and Ms. Hahn has a new baby."

Harry frowned. "What happened to her friends on the PTA committee?"

"All Mom said was that they've got problems of their own, and she didn't want to bother them. She told them she had it handled, but she can't. Mom's busy, too. She works all day, and has to do tons of stuff for us, and… Well, me and the boys said we'd help with the stage stuff, but Mom was trying to sew feathers on a turkey, and Mom doesn't sew. She's got to finish it all, and work with the third-graders, and Mr. Rem…"

Harry had forgotten how much he'd missed hearing Stan call him that, until the nickname slipped out.

"Third-graders are tough. The other classes are singing some songs, but Mom's gotta teach those third-graders the whole play. I mean, I just live with Stella and that's hard enough. Mom needs some help. And I thought, maybe you—" He shrugged.

"You thought maybe I could help?"

"I know you're busy here, and Mom says you're taking classes, but maybe you'd have some time?"

Everything in Harry wanted to jump at the excuse to spend time with Samantha, but he held himself back. "Stan, your mom thinks it might not be such a good idea for us to be friends."

"Because of me."

He saw the guilt in Stan's expression and hastened to reassure him. "Well, your mom loves you very much and cares about how you feel. Besides, your mom and I, we're both busy. I've got my own classes, and running this school, and your mom has you kids, work and the Thanksgiving Pageant. That's a lot for each of us."

"But you were seeing each other until I gave my mother problems."

Harry wasn't about to let the boy take the blame for everything. "Stan, this is about your mom and me, not you. Sometimes grown-ups might like each other, but still—" He shrugged. "Listen, you know I had a girl-friend for a long time, and we broke up before I moved here, but the thing is, I'm still hurting. And your mom's still hurting. And…"

Stan's expression would have told Harry that he knew he wasn't doing a good job of explaining things even if he didn't already know it.

"Mr. Rem, I don't get grown-ups. But I know my mom loves me, and that when I…"

Harry could see that whatever Stan was trying to say was hard for him. Thirteen-year-olds had a powerful sense of pride.

"When I acted like a baby, complaining 'cause Mom and you were friends, well, she stopped seeing you, 'cause she loves me. But Mr. Rem, I love her, and she misses you. I can tell. So, maybe you are busy, but maybe not too busy to give her a hand with the pageant?"

"And you'd be all right with that?" Harry asked.

"I've got lots of people to talk to. My mom, my dad now. My brothers and friends. Not really Stella so much, 'cause she's so little, but I've got lots of people. Even that shrink you made me talk to. Mom, she's just got us kids and her PTA friends. She was happier when she had you around, too. She misses you."

Harry knew that getting in any deeper with Samantha

was a mistake, for all the reasons they'd both gone over. He also knew that he wasn't quite strong enough to walk away from this opportunity. "So, I'll come help."

"That would be good. This afternoon, after school."

Harry stood and extended his hand. "Thanks, Stan. Your mom's lucky she has you to look out for her."

Stan shook his head. "I didn't do such a great job before, but I'm trying."

"That's all a man can do—try."

Stan started walking toward the door, and Harry said, "And Stan…?

The boy turned around.

"I'll try not to embarrass you in front of your friends again."

Stan shrugged. "I can take care of them, Mr. Rem."

Harry raised an eyebrow, not sure that Stan's taking-care-of would fall within what was permissible at school.

Stan grinned. "Not like I'd punch 'em or anything."

"I'm sure you wouldn't."

Stan hesitated and added, "Mom's coming today right after school," as if he wasn't sure he could trust Harry to remember.

"I won't forget, Stan. It might take me a bit to get all the end-of-the-day stuff done, but I'll be there."

Stan nodded, turned around and left.

Harry sat at his desk. He'd promised he'd help with the pageant preparations tonight, and he would. He missed Samantha. Missed her a lot, maybe more than he should.

Chapter Nine

As she faced the third-grade class, Samantha felt butterflies in her stomach, but she tried to ignore them. She was an adult—she could do this. "Hi, everyone."

The Erie Elementary gym did double duty as the auditorium, with a raised stage at one end. Samantha was standing in front of it, while the third-graders sat in a semicircle on the floor. Thankfully, she'd volunteered in Stella's class, so she knew most of the kids' names. "I think you all recognize me. I'm Mrs. Williams, Stella's mom. I'm going to help you with the pageant since Mrs. Tarbot is ill."

"Yeah, her stomach blew up," one girl, Mia, said.

"Well, it didn't actually blow up. Her appendix—"

"Exploded. Pow," Nate cried excitedly.

"Gross," exclaimed a group of girls in unison.

Samantha realized she was losing control, so she said loudly, "That's enough, class."

When the children got quieter, she started again. "Okay, let's talk about the show. Mrs. Tarbot picked out a poem this year that will be our play. I've made copies of it for all of you. You have two weeks to memorize it, but if you forget the lines, don't worry. We're all going to be reciting the poem together, and I'll have someone backstage to help you remember. Now we'll need to pick a few special roles, and everyone who doesn't get one of these will just wear their school clothes and sit on the sides of the stage. We need a mother, a father, a brother, a sister, a turkey, a pumpkin pie and a pilgrim. I thought—"

Every hand was raised high. Some kids had both hands raised. And J.C. Peters had gone beyond that and was standing, waving both hands and doing a little dance. Samantha tried to forget she was outnumbered thirty to one. "I thought, to be fair, we'd draw names from a hat and—"

"No," came a universal outcry, then individual children started arguing as to why he or she deserved a particular part more than the rest of the class, or why the child didn't want a part at all. Janey said something like, "But I've got basketball," while Samantha caught other bits such as, "I don't want to play the turkey," and "Dad says I have a big mouth."

"Kids. Kids," she pleaded.

"Everyone sit down and be quiet." She recognized the voice behind her. "I expect better from my school," Harry continued.

From the stage, Harry bent down to jump onto the gym floor. When he was standing next to her, she shot him a look of appreciation, and tried not to wonder why he was there.

"Mrs. Williams," he continued, "is volunteering and doing a lot more than she signed up for because Mrs. Tarbot isn't well. So, you all are going to show your appreciation by sitting down, listening and doing whatever Mrs. Williams asks." Harry looked at Samantha, and winked. "Mrs. Williams, would you like continue?"

She took a deep breath, noticing that Harry was so

close that all she could smell was his cologne. It wasn't overbearing, only the lightest of scents. Warm and slightly woodsy.

"Samantha?" Harry whispered.

She shook herself from her cologne-induced stupor and looked at the now quiet class. "Since there are no extra lines to learn—like I said, we'll all be reciting the poem together. The fairest way is to draw names for the roles," she repeated. "Everyone whose name isn't pulled from the hat will wear their normal play clothes to the pageant."

"But I want to wear my party dress," Mary called out.

"Mary, I didn't see a hand," Harry scolded gently.

The little blonde raised her hand, but didn't wait to be acknowledged as she again called out, "But I want to wear my party dress."

"Mary, if you want to wear a party dress, you can. Unless you're chosen for a role, then you'll have a special costume."

"Do you have all the names?" Hannah, also forgetting to raise her hand, asked.

"Ha—" Harry started to say, but Samantha ignored the hand-raising faux pas and answered, "Yes. I had a copy of the class list, so I wrote all the names on slips of paper and put them in this bag."

"Hey, you said our names would be in a hat," Theo insisted. But Theo had a bit of a lisp so it sounded more like, *Hey, you thed our nameth would be in a hat.*

"It's a saying," Samantha assured him. Of all the arguments she'd tried to prepare for, this wasn't one.

"Well, we want a hat," Theo maintained, and because the sentence lacked s's, it came out perfectly clear.

Samantha didn't have a hat and wasn't sure what to do now because it was clear from Theo's stubborn expression that he wasn't going to settle for a bag. "Theo, I—"

"I have a baseball hat in my office," Harry offered.

"I'll go get it, Mr. Rem," offered Stan, who'd been painting a piece of scenery.

Samantha had been surprised that Harry had appeared at the rehearsal, but she was beyond surprised that Stan had offered to help Harry. Her son was back in short order, baseball cap in hand. He purposefully didn't meet her gaze as they dumped the slips of paper from the bag into the hat.

With Harry's assistance, Samantha had the roles assigned. When Harry pulled the slip that said Stella Williams for the role of the mom, Stella jumped up, ran to Harry and threw herself in his arms, hugging him for all she was worth. "Thanks, Mr. Rem."

Harry looked flustered as he hugged the little girl back and assured her, "I didn't do anything but pull the slip."

Samantha had thought that handing out the roles would be a piece of cake, but by the time the task was completed, she was ready to call it a day. Unfortunately, parents wouldn't be arriving for another forty-five minutes. There was nothing left to do but get on with the practice and try not to think about why Harry Remington was there.

Samantha attempted to ignore him as she worked with the class on reading through the poem.

> "... 'Tis Thanksgiving morning, the kids are in bed
> And mom's in the kitchen hoping all will be fed.
> She's stuffing the turkey
> And kneading the rolls..."

Stella jumped up at the stuffing-the-turkey line, grabbed Jewel—who was to play the turkey—and seemed prepared to stuff her. But before she could do anything to poor Jewel, Samantha warned, "Stella, we're not acting anything yet, we're just learning the poem."

"Ah, Mom," Stella cried before plopping back into the semicircle.

Eventually, parents began arriving to pick up their kids. "Please, help your children learn the poem," Samantha called after each new batch of adults gathered up their third-graders and headed away from the gym.

Todd's mother, who'd barely left, returned. "Todd said you gave out parts and he didn't get one."

"I did. You see—"

"Todd's been acting in plays since he was Baby Jesus in the Christmas play when he was eighteen months. How could you overlook him for a role?"

"Mrs. Liekowski, I didn't hand out roles. I'm sure, had Mrs. Tarbot been here, she'd have known about Todd's abilities. Although I know the kids through Stella, I don't know them as well as a teacher would, so I did the only fair thing I could think of, I drew names."

"Todd said your daughter got a role." Mrs. Liekowski had the stubborn look of someone who wasn't going to let this go.

"Only because her name was drawn, not by some sort of parental nepotism, I assure you."

"Well, it all seems rather fishy to me. I'm going to complain to the principal. Maybe your daughter should give up her role so Todd can have it."

Harry waved from on the stage. "Hello, Mrs. Liekowski. I couldn't help but overhear. First, let me assure you that the drawing was absolutely fair. After all, it was my hat the names were pulled from. Second, I'm pretty sure if you asked Todd, he wouldn't be interested in Stella's role—"

"And I'm sure he would be. He's broken-hearted."

"Stella's playing the *mother* in our play," Samantha told the woman. "I have three boys myself, and I'm sure none of them would be willing to play a female role in a school production."

"Oh."

For a moment, Samantha thought that would be all there was to it, but Mrs. Liekowski said, "We could ask him."

"No." Harry jumped down from the stage. "I'm afraid I can't let Mrs. Williams do that. It would set a bad precedent, and there's no way she can get ready for the play and accommodate a potential merry-go-round of role trading."

"Oh."

That drew Mrs. Liekowski up short. "I guess I can see your point, Principal." And with that the woman was gone.

"My hero," Samantha said. She tried to pass it off as a joke, but truth be told, she was way too tired to have dealt as well as Harry had with a stage mom in the making.

"All part of the service," Harry told her. He went back to the stage, as Samantha waited for the rest of the parents to come claim their kids.

No other parents complained, but Samantha wasn't quite sure she was out of the woods. Finally, the only children left in the room were hers. "Okay, boys, finish the painting, and clean up. I need to go home."

Samantha might still have on her sensible nursing Crocs, but she had to get out of her scrubs and into some jeans. The thought of making something for dinner was almost too overwhelming to handle.

She saw Harry on the stage earnestly talking to the boys about the scenery they had been painting.

"Thanks for the help, Harry," she called.

She sure had appreciated this. She wasn't sure she'd

have survived Theo's no-hat crisis, along with Mrs. Liekowski's.

Harry returned the wave and walked out the door at the back of the stage that led into the first-floor hallway. Stan jumped from the stage onto the gym floor. "I asked Mr. Rem to come to dinner."

Stan's stance was almost defiant, as if he was waiting for Samantha to get upset and he was preparing to deal with it.

"You what?" She'd been shocked before, but really, this was akin to Stan informing her he was going to join the French Foreign Legion, or the girl's cheerleading squad.

"Mr. Rem said no," Stan added, glaring at her, as if it were her fault.

Samantha had been surprised, but admitted that for a split second, she'd hoped Harry had said yes, forcing her, out of politeness, to spend the evening with him.

"You should ask him," Stan continued. His back, if possible, was even more ramrod-straight.

"Harry and I decided we should keep our relationship professional. It was nice that he came here today, but it was because he's the principal, nothing more."

"You decided not to be friends anymore because of me."

When had Stan grown so astute?

"Honey, that's not the only reason. I love you enough to want you to be happy, but I'm also realistic enough to know that I deserve a life of my own, and if Harry and I were meant to stay friends, I'd have found some way to make you okay with that. The reality is that he's leaving and—"

"Mom, you're unhappy because you miss Harry."

How could she deny that? She did miss Harry, and that was just another reason why it was best to nip this in the bud, or else it was bound to hurt more when Harry left to go back to Ohio.

"Stan, it's for the best."

"Mom, I'm thirteen. Like you say, I'm not quite a grown-up, but I'm not a little kid anymore. You liked him as more than just a friend."

Harry was… She didn't know how to describe him. He wasn't a boyfriend. And he was more than just an old friend, or a new friend. He was potentially more than any of those definitions. Potentially more. That described what she and Harry were.

They were potentially more.

She couldn't say any of that to Stan, who was obviously confused enough, so she said, "Listen, don't worry about me. I'm all the way grown up and I can handle my friendships myself." She paused and added for good measure, "I'm fine."

"You miss him, Mom," he stubbornly insisted.

"Stan—"

"Mom, you know what you've always said about being a parent?"

What was it—quote Mom day? She'd never counted on having to watch her words, that someday they'd come back and bite her in the butt.

Stan didn't wait for her to respond. "You said you try to decide what to do with us by asking will it hurt? If we ask to stay up late and watch a movie, you let us if it's a weekend, 'cause we can sleep in the next day. If it's a weekday, you say no 'cause of school and we'd be tired the next day, but you tape it for us. And remember last Christmas?"

"The Christmas cookies?"

He nodded.

When would she ever learn? Not only her words, but

her actions were coming back to haunt her. It had seemed so innocent at the time. She'd had a ton of holiday cookies left over, and when the kids had begged to have one with their breakfast, she'd said, "No, let's have all of them for breakfast."

It had been such a hard holiday without Phillip there. She'd done what she could to make it special, and decided one breakfast of cookies in a lifetime of oatmeal wouldn't kill her kids. The Christmas cookie breakfast had rapidly become the thing legends are made out of.

"Yeah, and Seton threw up after it. He still says it's one of the coolest things ever. Then you made us promise if we had those cookies for breakfast, that we'd eat three fruits and three vegetables every day for two weeks."

"And you discovered you did like kiwis," she reminded Stan.

"Even though they're hairy. So that breakfast didn't hurt after all."

"No, you're right. To splurge every now and again is what makes life fun."

"Mom, Harry's going away before Christmas break. I was being a jerk about you guys being friends. I asked myself, what's it going to hurt? And it's not gonna hurt anything. Even if you liked him more than a friend, it would be all right. Dad has a girlfriend, and she's okay. I mean, Lois likes us and tries to get Dad to spend more time with us, so it's good that she's living with Dad. And, Mom, I don't like it when you're sad. You've been sad 'cause you miss Mr. Rem, and that's my fault for acting like a kid, instead of the oldest."

"Stan…" She was choked up and knew if she got all watery, Stan was going to be embarrassed, so she forced herself to be as unwatery as possible. "That's sweet. But even though you're the oldest, you are a kid. You don't have to worry about me. It's my job to worry about you."

"Yeah, but maybe sometimes I can worry, too, just a little? I mean, everyone needs someone to worry about them."

She'd held back the tears, but couldn't quite stop herself from reaching over and ruffling Stan's hair.

Stan, sensing he'd won the argument, pushed. "So, ask him to dinner."

Stan had a point. What would it hurt?

She did miss Harry, and he'd been very sweet to come help today.

Decision made, she said, "Fine. Help your brothers and sister clean up the mess, and let me go see if Mr. Remington has other plans." She paused. "Stan, I do love you, more than anything. Don't forget that, will you?"

"I won't, Mom."

She climbed the stairs to the stage feeling lighter than she had in days. Tracing Harry's steps, she arrived at his office door, which was open, so she walked in.

Suddenly felt nervous. "Hi, Harry, I… Well, Stan mentioned he'd invited you to dinner, but you'd said no. He seemed to think if I issued the invitation, you'd be more inclined to agree."

"Samantha, I thought you didn't want to spend any more time with me." He sounded wounded.

That had never been her intent. "Not wanting to spend time with you wasn't it at all. I really want to spend time with you—all the time we can manage—which ultimately could be the problem."

Harry shook his head. "Sam, I'm going to confess, I don't get it. You want to spend time with me, so you don't. Yet, here you are asking me to dinner despite that. What do I do, I ask you? Am I a good guy if I say yes, or a jerk?"

Her logic did seem convoluted. "Listen, Harry, I know you didn't ever want to get involved with another woman with kids, but Stan reminded me that we can't live in the past, or worry so much about the future that we forget the present. And at present, I'm here, you're here, and there's a dinner out there somewhere."

"And about the rest?" he asked.

"For tonight, let's just worry about eating. I skipped lunch today because the office was so swamped. Then I came right here after I got out, so I'm pretty convinced my stomach is eating itself, it's so hungry. There's no way I can untangle my thoughts until I have some food. Maybe after that, if we both put our heads together, we can figure it out. I do know one thing, I did miss you."

Harry rose from his chair, sporting a big grin. "Well, we can't have your stomach eating itself. I'm sure we can find something better. Let's go."

HARRY TOOK SAMANTHA'S suggestion and forgot about the past and the future, and tried to live thoroughly in the present.

And it was a great present.

They went back to Patti's Pizza, which was conveniently close and was definitely what the kids would enjoy.

"We're almost regulars," Seton announced, as he led them to the same table they'd sat in before.

"Pretty soon someone will be yelling, 'Hey, Norm,' when we come in," Samantha joked.

Since *Cheers* was well before the kids' time, the only one who got the joke was Harry, who'd laughed easily. He liked having a small inside joke with her.

Who was he kidding, he liked everything about her.

They ate and joked, and unlike their other meals, Stan joined in and seemed to enjoy himself. Harry wasn't sure what to make of the change, just as he wasn't sure what to do about Samantha's invitation.

The meal finished, Harry said, "I guess I better get going."

"Mr. Rem, could you come home with us?" Stella asked. "Mommy lets me play outside 'til dark, and maybe you could push me on the swing for a while."

"I'm afraid it will be dark before we'd get back to your house," Harry replied.

"But if you come with me, Mommy would still let me go out for a few minutes. We have a big backyard light," Stella wheedled.

"And we have ice cream in the fridge, and we could have dessert," Seton chirped up. "If Mom says so," he hastened to add.

"Mom will say so. We all ate some salad," Shane jumped in with the kind of certainty that only an eleven-year-old could muster.

Harry looked at Samantha and shrugged, not sure how she'd want him to answer.

She seemed to understand his dilemma. "Mr. Rem might have other plans, still Harry, we'd love to have you join us for some ice cream and swinging if you're able to, if not, we'll understand." There was warning in her voice, telling the kids they weren't to whine if his answer was no.

Rather than no, Harry found himself saying, "I'd love to."

AND THAT'S WHAT THEY DID. Some swinging, followed by ice cream sundaes all around. Stan even asked Harry for some help with his algebra homework.

Harry kept thinking he should go, but couldn't seem to manage it, which was why he was still at the

Williamses' house when Samantha had disappeared upstairs to get Stella ready for bed.

Harry and the boys were watching wrestling on television, when Stella came down in her pajamas. "Mr. Rem, would you like to read me my story tonight?" she asked. "Mommy said it would be all right."

Something melted in him as he looked at the little girl in her pink nightgown. "Sure, I'd love to."

Harry was soon sitting in the pink bedroom reading a book about ten monkeys in a bed.

"No, no," Stella hollered. "You've got to sing it." She hummed the tune.

"Are you sure you want me to sing?" he asked Stella. "I mean, I don't want to give you nightmares…it's bad."

The little girl giggled and nodded, so Harry obliged.

Stella's clapping interrupted him. "You sing real good, Mr. Rem," she said, then snuggled closer as he finished the book, humming along with him until the end of the story.

"I'm glad you're back, Mr. Rem," Stella murmured as he finished the story.

Harry leaned down and kissed her forehead. "I'm glad to be back, Stella."

He hurried out of the room and simply stood in the hall. He had missed not just the kids, but Samantha, too. Everything seemed… He searched for a way to explain it. Brighter. Yes, everything seemed brighter with her around.

Samantha peeked in at Stella, then shut the door gently behind her.

The murmur of the television drifted up the stairs, punctuated by the occasional whoop of one of the boys.

Harry wasn't sure what to say, so he settled for, "Thanks for tonight. I should probably be going…."

Even as the words left his mouth, he realized he didn't want to. His place was too quiet.

Samantha nodded. "You probably should, but before you do, we could do this…."

He didn't have time to be surprised, as her lips touched his. He wrapped his arms around her, loving how she felt against him. Loving the taste of her, the feel of her. Wanting this moment to go on, and on…

"Mom, Seton lost the remote, and the wrestling match is over and we want to change the channel," Stan called from the bottom of the stairs.

"I didn't lose it," Seton retorted.

"I guess it's too much to ask that they get up and change the channel manually, or get up and look for the remote?" Samantha called back. She turned to Harry. "Sorry."

"Should we talk—" he started to ask.

"No. We should go find the remote before they start a riot."

"Sam?"

"Listen, Harry. Nothing's changed. We both have baggage and you're still leaving. Going back to your old school, your family and friends, your Saturday morning basketball games…"

Harry knew he should be chomping at the bit to get back to Columbus, but for the life of him, he didn't want to be anywhere but here, with Samantha.

"I know, but—"

"And I'm taking my own advice. I'm going to forget about the past, stop worrying about tomorrow and live in the moment. And at the moment, I'd like to invite you out this weekend. My ex has the kids and it would be just the two of us with no interruptions," she added.

"Sami, are you sure?"

"No, but I'm sick to death of second-guessing myself. I'd really like to spend the weekend with you. I know I can get by on my own. This last year has taught me that

I don't need anyone to lean on. But Harry, I simply like having you around. I could push you away now, try to save myself some pain when you go, but then I'd miss out on these last few weeks with you. That's just dumb. So, what do you say, want a date this weekend?"

He nodded, what had to be a goofy grin grew on his face. "What do you have in mind? We could go away for the weekend."

She shook her head. "There's Grunge and Marmalade. So if you don't mind, it would be easier to just stay in."

"I don't mind at all," he assured her.

"Mom, we don't want to watch this," Shane called again.

"A weekend with no interruptions," she told him as she started down the stairs. "Oh, my goodness, just look at that. Three boys on the couch. That's six legs and not one of them appears to be broken."

The but-moms started. Harry smiled as he listened to them. He wasn't sure what brought about Samantha's change of heart, but he wasn't going to argue. He would simply take her advice and forget about the past, stop worrying about the future and just enjoy the moment, because right now the moment looked pretty near perfect.

And this weekend looked to be the same.

Chapter Ten

The week should have sped by.

Each morning Samantha left home, dropped the kids off at school, hurried to work, then back to the school for pageant practice. There, she ran lines with thirty kids, and choreographed the staging, as well. She fit costumes, sorted out the scenery and drafted a program. Then dinner, homework, bedtimes. It was grueling and she didn't feel as if she had a minute to catch her breath...except when she was in Harry's arms.

That first time he'd touched her she felt as if something had been rekindled in her, and that it was growing as they spent more time together.

Every afternoon, Harry stayed to help with rehearsals, then had dinner with them.

Stan still seemed okay with Harry being around, and the other kids were thrilled. They thrived on Harry's attention, and he lavished it on them, as much as he did on her. It was as if a floodgate had been opened and things she hadn't known she'd been holding on to were finally free to come to the surface.

It wasn't just the sexual tension, although that was a part of it. It was the sharing. Homework, games, his simply watching a show with them.

She warned herself not to get too dependent, too close, and to harden her heart. But every time she saw him roughhousing with the boys, or reading to Stella, she melted.

By Friday, she was a basket case of nerves.

She wasn't really second-guessing her invitation; however, last night as she shaved her legs in anticipation of tonight, it had struck her that no man had seen her post-baby body except her ex. And Phillip had been there as the changes gradually stole away her girlish figure and replaced it with something more…well, padded. Things had rearranged, and stretched. Time had seen to that.

Her stomach sucking had helped. There was definitely a hardness to her abs that had been missing since her teens. Unfortunately, the muscles were covered with a soft cushion that was new.

Friday afternoon, she couldn't seem to keep her place in the poem as the kids recited it.

"Samantha, are you okay?" Harry finally asked.

She wasn't. She needed to be talked down, and there were only two people she trusted to do that for her. "Harry, do you mind running through the poem again with the kids while I go make a call?"

"Sure. No problem."

Samantha hurried out into the hall and made a quick, emergency conference call to Michelle and Carly.

"Sorry to bother you guys, but I need to talk," she began.

"Sure," came their stereo reply.

"Problems with the pageant?" Carly asked. "I can be there next week——"

"No. Problems with…" Samantha felt a stab of embarrassment. "I…you see, I'm about to have Harry *over* tonight. The kids are going to their Dad's and—"

"Oh, *over*," Carly said with the proper emphasis on the word.

"Yeah. And the problem is, I haven't had a man *over* in years." She went on to explain her pre-baby, post-babies predicament

Michelle's voice was soft with sympathy. "You're scared."

"Not scared exactly, more nervous." Samantha caught herself in the lie. "Yes, scared. I'm scared out of my gourd. That's why I called. It couldn't wait until our next meeting."

"I thought you and Harry decided to back off?" Carly asked.

"We did. It didn't stick." She peeked through the door and saw Harry, surrounded by third-graders reciting,

"She's stuffing the turkey
And kneading the rolls.
She's mashing the potatoes
And filling the bowls.
The oven is heating and so are the pots
To fill all the family, her husband and tots."

"He's helping the third-graders with their lines now. How can I resist a man who not only reads bedtime stories to my daughter and puts up swings in the yard, but doesn't mind leading thirty kids in a Thanksgiving poem?"

"Sam, the only thing you've mentioned is how good Harry is with kids. There has to be more to it than that, or it's not worth it," Michelle ventured.

"More to it?" Samantha repeated. "I wish that was all there was to how I feel about Harry. If it was just that he's great with kids, it would be easy to do this, to know I'm going to have him over, and he's still going to leave in a few weeks. There's no rational explanation. He's nice. He's smart. I've never seen him kick a dog. But there are a lot of men who fall into that category."

"Maybe not as many as you think," Carly muttered.

Samantha laughed. "Okay, maybe not. Those reasons are a part of, but not all of, my attraction to Harry. He touches me. Something I thought died a long time ago came back to life the moment he placed his hand on my shoulder, oh, so platonically. Being with him makes me realize how hollow my relationship with Phillip had become. Everything we did centered around the kids. We lost us somewhere along the line. Sometimes I wonder if we really had an us because with Harry, it's there. There's an *us*. The kids are part of it, but there would be an *us* without the kids. There's an indescribable connection. I tried to ignore it, to pretend it away, but I couldn't. Even though I know it won't last, I want more with him."

"Then from everything you've said about him, if Harry feels even a percentage of what you feel, he's not going to notice that your body's been lived in. He's only going to see you, Sam. And you are one of the most beautiful ladies I've ever known," Michelle reassured her. "If it's right, it will be all right. Does that make sense?"

"I'd say something as moving and brilliant," Carly said, "but I'd never manage it, so I'll just say ditto."

Samantha laughed again. Some of the unbearable pressure seemed to have eased. "Thanks, guys."

"You call again if you need us," Michelle said.

"Any time you need us," Carly added. "And you might want to warn Harry that if he hurts you, we'll track him down."

"I'm going into this with my eyes wide open. I know he's not here to stay, and I also know that the pain of him leaving is worth this."

She promised to call them next week, and hurried back to the gym, feeling much better.

> *"...then Mother sat down at her holiday chair,*
> *And looked at the meal she made with such care.*
> *She realized Thanksgiving wasn't the rolls,*
> *The turkey, the stuffing or heaping bowls.*
> *She looked at the faces of Joe, Bob and Ann,*
> *She looked at her husband, she looked at her friends.*
> *Thanksgiving's a day to remember to start*
> *Saying thanks for the things that are near to our*
> *heart."*

As if on cue, Harry turned around and looked at her, his smile as warm as his eyes.

It was all she could do not to walk over and throw her arms around him, to tell him that he meant more to her than his attributes she could list. He was more than a man who was good with kids—good with her kids. He was more than his intelligence, or his caring. He was... Harry was just more.

When he looked at her like that, with those knowing, warm eyes, she forgot that she was nervous about her body, nervous about a first time with a man. She forgot everything except the fact that Harry was more.

She didn't dare go any further in trying to define what she felt for him, because if she did—if she put a name to the more-ness—it would hurt too much to let him go.

He saw her as a rebound woman, someone he liked, and maybe cared for. But she saw him as more.

"Samantha, are you okay?" Harry called.

She gave herself a mental shake and forced a smile. On her approach, she replied, "I'm fine. How about we run through the play one more time before everyone's parents come?"

"You sure everything's okay?" Harry asked softly.

She smiled. "Everything's fine."

She recited the poem again with the kids, while Harry helped the boys with the set. Parents started trickling in and she made sure all of them got next week's schedule as they gathered kids and backpacks and left for their weekends.

Phillip came in, a tall, lean blonde in tow. "Hi, Samantha."

"Hi, Phillip."

The woman with her ex didn't wait for introductions. "Hi, Samantha. I'm Lois." Her expression said she was nervous and unsure of her reception.

Samantha nodded reassuringly. "I assumed. I'm glad I finally get to meet you."

"I thought it was time. I know if some woman was spending weekends with my kids, I'd want to meet her and check her out." She offered her hand.

Samantha shook it and said, "The kids have mentioned you so frequently and had such good things to say about you. It's nice to have the chance to thank you for taking care of them."

"See, I told you. Samantha and I are going to get along fine." Lois elbowed Phillip, who grinned at her good-natured teasing. "I keep telling him I'm always right, but he doesn't believe me. Someday he will."

Samantha chuckled, liking Phillip's girlfriend more than she'd have imagined she could.

Stella spotted her father and screamed, "Daddy," as she ran across the gym floor and threw herself into his arms.

"We'll be down in a minute, Dad," Seton called from the stage.

While Phillip was busy listening to Stella's litany

about her week at school, Lois handed Samantha a piece of paper. "I've put my numbers on it, work, too. If you think of any questions, I'd be happy to answer them and put your mind at ease. Phillip said not to come on too strong. I'm not looking for us to be best friends, but I'd like the two of us to be friendly. So, this isn't me trying to force anything, but rather me just trying to make things as easy on you and on the kids as I can. I'm hoping I'm here to stay." She glanced at Phillip and Stella, and there was a look in her eyes that Samantha recognized.

She suspected she had the same look when she saw Harry.

Samantha took the paper. "I think I'm hoping you are, too."

"Maybe we could do coffee sometime? You can fill me in on what sort of rules you keep at your house, and I'll try my best to keep them at ours, as well. The kids need consistency, and they need to know they're loved. I'll confess, I'm learning to love them a lot."

"And they sound as if they're learning to love you, too. Coffee sounds great. Maybe over the Thanksgiving holiday?"

"It's a date." Lois's relief was evident on her face.

Phillip came over, Stella wrapped around his neck, and hanging down his back.

"We're going to do coffee over the holiday break," Lois said without preamble.

She kissed Phillip's cheek.

Samantha smiled. "Phillip, we all have to put the kids first. And I'm looking forward to getting to know Lois better."

They walked as a group to her car, where she pulled out the kids' overnight bags. She kissed her children, even Stan, who groaned. "I'll see you guys Sunday night. Call and say goodnight, okay?"

"They'll call," Lois promised. She herded the kids and Phillip toward his car.

Harry had hung back, giving Samantha some time to herself as he locked up the school. "Well, I couldn't help but notice she seems…energetic."

Samantha grinned. "That's a good word. She also seems nice. I'm glad for Phillip, and even more, I'm glad for my kids. Lois seems genuine in wanting to do what's best for them. And kids can't have too many people caring about them."

"That's not how these things normally work. People hate their exes."

"I don't. Phillip walking out wasn't all on him. At some point, we'd both stopped trying. How can I hate him for being the first one to realize how…well, how not happy we were? I don't approve of how he left, and I really hate what he put the kids through, but he's back on track now and he's trying. And part of that is thanks to Lois. I should get along with her for that reason alone."

Harry was grinning at her with a knowing look on his face.

"I'm no saint," she protested. "And I've heard you talk about Teresa. You don't hate her, either."

"Guilty. And although I'm over her, I do miss Lucas."

"So, call and see if she'll let him visit."

"You think?"

"I think."

He smiled. "Maybe I will." He stepped closer and pulled her into his arms. "You're a very special person, Samantha."

"You, too, Harry."

"So, since it's just the two of us very special people

here, why don't we get some dinner and then…" He wiggled his eyebrows up and down.

She nodded. "And then…"

HARRY COULD TELL SAMANTHA was nervous. He totally understood. It might not be macho to admit it, but he was nervous, too. He knew what tonight's invitation meant, and it wasn't that he didn't want to be with Samantha, but he didn't want to mess up what they already had. He didn't want to hurt her when he left. And he was going back to his job and life in Columbus soon.

Why? a small voice inside him whispered. He could stay, and give himself more time with Samantha?

He ignored the voice. He cared about Samantha, and he cared about her kids. If he were honest about it, he knew he could easily fall for the lot of them, and he knew that if he let himself believe, and then lost them all… No, he wasn't going through that again. He and Samantha had set their ground-rules. Maybe he should call tonight off?

He probably should, but he wasn't sure he had that much willpower. He wanted her. There was something about her that touched him.

Samantha spilled her water at dinner, then thwacked her head getting into the car. By the time they reached her house, she'd gone from jittery to practically jumping out of her skin.

She opened the door and just stood in the foyer, as if unclear what to do next.

He took her hand and drew her into the living room. "Sami, it's me. No, it's us. It will work itself out, so relax." He led them to the couch, patted a cushion and sat down. He immediately jumped back up and pulled the Transformer from the crack in the cushions.

"Oh, Harry, I'm sorry. I should have taken more time to clean up. I mean—"

"Sam."

Her head jerked up and she was quiet.

"Samantha, it's okay. Whatever happens, or doesn't happen, it's okay. Really."

"Don't you see, I can't relax. The last time I did something like this for the first time, the first Bush was in office, or maybe Clinton had just started his presidency. Either way, I was in my teens and had a size-ten body that hadn't carried four kids. I don't know how to do this—"

Harry didn't know what to do, what to say, so he simply leaned forward and kissed her. Kissed her like he meant it. Minutes went by, before he pulled back. "It's been a long time for me, as well. Clinton was in his second term when Teresa and I got together," Harry teased her softly. "But I'm happy to report, it seems to be coming back to me. How about you? Still nervous?"

"I know I shouldn't be, but yes."

"Maybe you'd forget about nerves if I started…" He kissed her again, slowly. They had the house to themselves, so there was no rush. There would be no interruptions. He felt her tension ease as she moved closer to him, relaxing in his arms. He deepened the kiss, and his hands began to explore her body. She was all curves and soft invitation, as tantalizing as her kisses. He lost himself in the sensation of Samantha. Lost himself in the feel of her, the taste of her, the rhythm that they were finding together.

After a while, their shirts came off, and the feel of her pressed against him, skin to skin, was almost too much.

"What if we take this upstairs?" he asked.

"Yes." As she stood, she reached for her shirt and tried to cover herself.

"Don't," he said. "I love looking at you. I can't believe you don't know how beautiful you are."

She smiled. "Beautiful might be stretching it, but, Harry, the way you're looking at me right now, I feel like maybe I'm close."

"More than close, Sami. You're lush, curvaceous, sensual—"

SAMANTHA LAUGHED AS SHE led him up the stairs. "You're a walking thesaurus, Harry Remington."

"I can keep going," he assured her. "Voluptuous, delightful, sexy as hell—"

"I'm feeling better, you can stop now."

"Don't you see, I don't want to stop. Sami, you're so beautiful. I wish I could let you see yourself through my eyes. I wish you could know how truly lovely you are."

She turned and looked at him. And there, in his eyes, she didn't see teasing, she didn't see him wanting to calm her. She saw the truth, that Harry did see her as beautiful. And she felt it. She felt as if she were truly a sensuous, gorgeous woman.

She opened her bedroom door. "You're insane."

"About you."

She chuckled. "Maybe, but you're nuts in general, definitely."

He watched her as she took off her pants, his eyes were filled with warm appreciation. He waited until she was done, then took off his own, and took her into the bed. All her worries, all her inhibitions were gone.

Together they found a cadence that was entirely their own, and when they finished, Samantha realized that she felt whole. It wasn't just Harry, it was who she was when she was with Harry.

In Harry's arms, she felt completely herself.
She felt healed.
She felt beautiful.

Chapter Eleven

"Mom, Mom, Mom, Mom…" came the litany somewhere near Samantha's right ear, pulling her from her dreams.

Dreams of last weekend. One entire uninterrupted weekend with Harry while the kids were with their father. She and Harry had stayed in her bedroom mostly. They'd ordered their meals in, watched old movies and a football game and made love. Suddenly, she felt herself slipping back into her dreams, but that persistent voice continued, "Mom, Mom, Mom…"

Slowly, she forced her eyelids open. It was slow work. "Huh?"

"Mom, come on, get up. It's Tuesday. The pageant's today, and you said you'd do my hair, and then you've got to come to school with me, and then we've got to get everyone in the classroom dressed in their costumes, and then—"

"Coffee," she interrupted, glancing at the clock, which read the obscene time of six fifty-six. "Mommy needs coffee before you tell me one more *and then*."

"I'll go wake up the boys." Stella raced from her room.

Samantha closed her eyes again, just for a minute. She found the older she got the more time her body needed to ease itself from sleep to wakefulness. Today it was particularly hard to pull herself from her Harry-inspired dreams.

Slowly, she managed it, and her mind started to kick into gear, listing everything she had to get done before the eleven-o'clock pageant. The list was Energizer Bunny-ish because it kept going and going and going. She knew she had to get up and be going, too.

She pulled back the covers and was just about to sit up when Stella screamed, "Mommy, come on."

Samantha showered and dressed in record time. Feeling slightly more human, she stumbled down the stairs, dodged the tangle of gaming handset cords and stepped over a pile of pillows and blankets that Stella had used as a makeshift nest last night. She and Miss Ruby were pretending to be baby birds and were trying to get their mother, Marmalade, to feed them worms.

Samantha could smell the coffee as she walked into the kitchen and gave mental thanks to whoever thought of making programmable coffeemakers. She was just about to pour a cup, when Marmalade started with her I-need-to-go-out-this-minute bark.

Setting the coffee carafe down, Samantha went to the back door, let the dog out into her, thankfully, fenced-in backyard, and Grunge dashed out, as well.

She knew it was an omen. Today was not going to be a good day.

Unfortunately, there was no calling in sick or hiding out in her house. She had a Thanksgiving Pageant to put on.

"Kids, the cat got out."

Four sets of feet came thundering into the kitchen and ran out the back door. "Grunge, Grunge," they called. Marmalade, thinking it was a game, joined in, yapping happily, not caring it wasn't quite seven-thirty in the morning.

Her neighbors were going to love her.

Somehow, Samantha managed to get Grunge and Marmalade in the house, do Stella's hair and have everyone to school by eight minutes after eight. "Run. The late bell is at eight ten," she called, dropping them at the front door, then driving up and down the narrow street, looking for a parking place.

Parallel parking took a few minutes since it wasn't one of Samantha's most well-honed skills. And with the coffee she'd been longing for since waking up in hand, Samantha trudged into the school. How on earth was she going to get the stage set up, all the kids in costume and in place?

One step at a time, she told herself firmly.

She'd finished *How to Be Happy Without Really Trying* last night and the parting paragraph had read… *Happiness is within our reach, it simply requires that we proceed one step at a time. Cultivate optimism. Accept your right to be happy. Reconcile your past—it brought you here. Pursue your dreams. One step at a time.*

That's what this fall had been—a series of steps.

Finding friends in Michelle and Carly.

Finding Harry.

Even knowing that Harry was leaving, she'd found something in his arms. When he'd looked at her, he'd seen her. Not her stretch marks, or padding. He'd seen her. And he'd helped her see herself.

How many times had she told the kids that Phillip's leaving hadn't had anything to do with them? She believed that. But there was always a quiet whisper in the corner of her mind asking if his leaving were her fault. No…

Phillip hadn't left because of her.

She thought of Harry's descriptions of her. Lush, curvaceous, sensual, voluptuous, delightful, sexy as hell…

She was Samantha Burger Williams. A nurse. A mother. A friend. She was the organizer of Thanksgiving pageants. She was Harry's lover.

It would hurt when he left, but he'd given her a gift of finding herself.

She was going to be fine.

Feeling empowered, she hurried to the stage and started tugging the backdrop into place. The boys had done a great job painting a kitchen and dining-room scene. It was big though, and heavy. She dragged it, an inch at a time, across the stage.

"Hey, I can give you a hand with that," Carly called. "I still feel guilty you didn't let us help."

"I knew I could call you if I needed you, but we had everything under control. The kids made the scenery, and Harry was here, too." She smiled at the thought of him. Turning to Michelle, Samantha asked, "How are things with Brandon?"

"He seems to have stopped trying to find his father. He's accepted my offer—we'll look for him when Bran's eighteen." She looked around the stage. "So what can we do?"

"Let's finish setting up the stage, then we can get the kids into their costumes."

The work went faster with Michelle and Carly's assistance. It was almost nine when Harry arrived. Samantha was nearby, putting out the costumes, while Michelle and Carly were organizing the chairs around the dining-room table. She glanced up and smiled.

"I would have gotten here sooner, but all hell broke loose in the office. I'm here now, what do you need?"

"Well, there is one thing I could use."

"Oh, what's that?"

"This."

One step at a time, that's what the book said. Right now she was accepting that she deserved happiness, and the next step to getting it was to kiss Harry. As her lips touched his, she discovered she was right…it made her very happy.

"Ahem," came the very distinct sound of someone clearing their throat.

Samantha turned around and found her two friends looking at her and Harry and smiling in a totally knowing way.

Samantha decided to ignore what they'd seen. "Hi, guys. Ready for your next job?"

Samantha saw Harry eyeing her two friends. She was pretty sure he'd decided retreat was the best choice because he said, "Sounds like you have everything under control. I'll finish dousing the fires in my office," then hurried away.

"Fires?" Carly asked, eyeing Samantha. "That's an apt description of the two of you."

"It wasn't a fire…just a nice friendly warmth. It's embarrassing to be caught fawning all over him like some schoolgirl with a crush."

"That wasn't embarrassing. It was cute," Michelle said, a hint of wistfulness in her voice.

"Cute?" Carly countered. "It was hot."

A sound that was equivalent to that of a herd of elephants drowned out the rest of Michelle and Carly's teasing.

"I think the kids are here," Samantha said loudly.

It was a whirlwind of activity, and nerves prompted a last minute run-through of lines.

The parents arrived.

"Mommy, is Daddy and Lois out there?" Stella asked in what was supposed to be a stage whisper and ended up sounding like a bullhorn.

"Yes. They're over by the street side of the gym. Now, go get in your place before the curtain opens."

Samantha had the script in hand, ready to prompt as needed, and the entire class was in place.

"Can I have your attention?" Harry spoke into the microphone at the front of the gym.

Samantha could hear the fourth-graders start to sing their Thanksgiving song, standing in front of the stage. The third-graders were in their places on the stage itself, hidden from the audience by the still-closed curtain.

Samantha felt as jittery as if she were the one going on the stage. "Okay, everyone," she called. "Here we go." She ducked behind the backdrop.

The last song ended and the audience grew quiet. Harry continued, "Now, for the main event, I'd like to introduce our third grade as they present Thanksgiving at the Table."

Slowly, the curtain drew back.

"As Halloween and October ends,
Thoughts of some dinners with turkey begin.

Samantha knew that Michelle and Carly were doing their part as children showed up on stage right on cue.

All the practice was paying off as the kids moved flawlessly through the production.

"She's stuffing the turkey
And kneading the rolls.
She's mashing the potatoes
And filling the bowls.
The oven is heating and so are the pots
To fill all the family, her husband and tots."

Stella was supposed to run across the stage carrying a big metal roasting pan, and put it in the cardboard oven. Instead of going behind the table to the oven, like they'd practiced, Stella went in front. Samantha wanted to call out a warning that Stella was awfully close to the edge of the stage, but before she could, Harry darted out from somewhere on the gym floor and said, "Behind the table, Stella," and hurried back to the shadows.

Stella laughed, turned around and went behind the table, the kids never missed a beat with their reciting.

"...in the oven, all warm and glowing.

Samantha released a breath she hadn't been aware she'd been holding.

Harry had saved the day, but the day was coming when he'd no longer be around to help with plays or forestall mishaps.

He was leaving.

At first there had been a sort of comfort, knowing that what she had with Harry was going to be short-lived.

That it had an expiration date.

Now, thinking about him leaving brought no comfort, only a decidedly uncomfortable pain somewhere in the vicinity of her heart. It wasn't that she couldn't get by without Harry. She knew she could.

The fact was, she didn't want to.

The play was proceeding without any further incidents.

"...then Mother sat down at her holiday chair,
And looked at the meal she made with such care.
She realized Thanksgiving wasn't the rolls,
The turkey, the stuffing or heaping bowls.
She looked at the faces of Joe, Bob and Ann,

She looked at her husband, she looked at her friends.
Thanksgiving's a day to remember to start
Saying thanks for the things that are near to our
heart."

Near and dear to her heart. That described Harry to a tee.

She cared for him.

A lot.

The third-graders stayed in place on the stage, as the first- and second-grade classes walked onto the floor in front of the stage and sang their closing Thanksgiving song.

"We are thankful for everyone here, and those who
are far away.
We are thankful for those who must go, and thankful
for those who will stay."

Thankful, Samantha rolled the word on her tongue. She was thankful for the time she'd had with Harry. She wished it could last longer, still she'd simply accept it and be thankful for the time they had left.

THE CLASSES ALL LINED up and took a group bow. Well, the group was divided into about three different parts, all bowing a little off from where they should have been. But it was actually an endearing attempt, and the audience showed its appreciation with thundering applause.

When the noise quieted down, Jeb stepped center stage with a huge bundle of roses in his hands. "The third grade wants ta thank Mrs. Williams. She worked really hard on the play. Come on out, Mrs. Williams," he called as he wiped his perpetually runny nose on his sleeve.

Samantha didn't move for a minute, then as more and more kids started calling, "Mrs. Williams," she forced her leaden feet forward, and took the flowers from Jeb.

"Thank you," she said to the class, then hurried offstage, as the curtain closed. She set the flowers on a table, then spoke to the kids. "Wow, you were fantastic! Mrs. Tarbot is going to be so proud of you when she hears how brilliantly you did. Now, let's everyone get in line and be ready for Ms. Hahn to come and get you. If you're wearing a costume and need help getting it off, you can see me, or Mrs. Lewis or Ms. Hamilton."

Bedlam was the kindest description of the chaos of thirty kids trying to line up, take off costumes while chattering about their fun performance.

"Mommy, Mommy, did you see me?" Stella danced from foot to foot, too filled with excitement to stand still.

"I did, Stella, my bella."

"I was wonderful." Stella hugged herself and twirled happily. "I didn't make any mistakes or nothin'."

Samantha didn't mention her near fall off the stage. "You were perfectly wonderful."

"Can I stay here with you?"

"No. Remember, Daddy and Lois are going to take you for the rest of the afternoon to celebrate?" The end of the pageant marked the beginning of Thanksgiving vacation.

"Oh, yeah," Stella said brightly. "I bet they thought I was wonderful, too, don't you?"

"I'm sure they did."

"Tomorrow we're baking for Thanksgiving?"

Samantha nodded. "Yes. I'll need my helper."

"That's me."

"You're right, that's you." She leaned down and kissed her daughter.

She felt a moment of complete and absolute

mother's love. She watched Stella run off and join her class. Samantha was lucky. She might lose Harry soon, but she had her kids. She had herself. That would be enough.

The third grade marched back to their classroom to retrieve their coats and bookbags.

Samantha was heading toward Michelle and Carly, to thank them for taking the afternoon off to help, when Harry came up to her.

"Mrs. Williams, can I see you for a minute?" Harry asked in his most principalish tone.

She followed him to the least noisy corner of the stage, hidden behind the curtains. "I wondered if you'd let me take you to a celebratory late lunch?"

"I'd love it. And I suspect I have you to thank for the flowers."

"Given all you've done the last few weeks, it's the least I could do. It was a great production, Sami."

She could see that he was going to kiss her, and she realized that soon he'd be gone and there would be no more kisses. Once, she'd have been tempted to pull back, but at this moment, she wanted to savor every last instant with Harry, so she kissed him full on for all she was worth.

Harry seemed surprised and shot her a questioning look, but before he could say anything, someone screamed from the hall. "I'd better go. See you in a few minutes," he said quickly.

Samantha returned to find Carly and Michelle waiting.

"You okay?" Michelle asked.

"I'm fine." Harry's leaving would hurt, but she'd get over it and keep going. "Just fine."

HARRY KNEW SOMETHING was wrong, although he couldn't put his finger on what exactly. Samantha had been quiet—too quiet—throughout their lunch. She kept giving him these sad looks, which he couldn't quite figure out. She should be giddy with excitement that the pageant was not only a huge success, but also that it was over.

He'd followed her to her house, and she opened the door to Marmalade's loud, enthusiastic greetings. "Make yourself at home while I put the dog outside."

He went into the chaotic living room and couldn't help but smile. He liked that the house looked lived in. That Samantha was more concerned with comfort than a designer atmosphere.

He cleared a line of dolls off the couch, and noticed that Ruby was there. He wondered if Samantha realized Stella had forgotten Ruby. Maybe they could run it over to Phillip's?

Marmalade bounded into the living room, deftly dodging the impressive remains of a blanket tent as she hurried over to the couch to greet him.

"Hey, Marm." He petted the rather ugly dog's head. "Stella forgot Ruby. Will it be a problem?"

He caught Samantha eyeing the now doll-filled chair before taking a seat on the couch.

"No, she'll be fine. They're not staying overnight, only spending the evening."

"Oh, well, that's good." It got quiet, and he wasn't sure what to say. Samantha gave him another of those sad looks. Before he could ask her why she was unhappy, his cell phone rang. He pulled it from his pocket and checked the number. "I have to take this."

He got up off the couch, and moved toward the front window as he flipped the phone open. "Hi, bud. How was the last day of school?"

Harry offered an occasional, "Really," or, "Wow," as he listened to Lucas's recounting of his week. Harry missed these moments. Last year, in Columbus, Lucas would hang out in Harry's office after his last class, and ride home with him. That car trip had been a highlight of Harry's day, hearing the ins and outs, complaints about tests, about kids in his class. Glancing over to see Lucas blush as he talked about a girl he liked.

The feeling of impotence, knowing there was nothing he could do about the circumstances, hit.

"And Harry, guess what?"

He got himself under control and asked, "What?"

"Mom says maybe I can come to Columbus sometime soon."

In the distance, Harry heard Teresa's voice. "That's not what I said, Lucas."

"Well, she said maybe."

"I'd like that," Harry assured Lucas, trying not to think about what an understatement that was. Like it? He'd hold on to the possibility when he got back to Columbus. He glanced at Samantha, who was studiously eyeing a magazine, trying to give him privacy. Actually, he'd be missing a lot more than Lucas when he got back to Columbus.

"Mom wants ta talk to you, okay, Harry?"

He forced himself to concentrate on the conversation at hand. "That's fine, Lucas. I'm glad you called. I'm here, anytime."

"Thanks, Harry."

Harry could hear the phone being jostled, then Teresa's voice came on the line. "Harry?"

"Hi, Teresa."

"How are you?" There was genuine concern in her voice.

"Good." And as he said the word, he realized he was. Talking to Teresa didn't hurt like it once had. There was just the slightest hint of poignant remembrance, but no pain at all. "Much better, as a matter of fact."

"I'm glad. About what Lucas said…"

"Yes?"

"He's been begging to visit. I know he misses you, and you must miss him."

"I do. More than you know."

"I'm not sure yet how to make this work. Thinking about being without him—even temporarily—hurts, which only makes me understand how much pain it must be causing you. Harry, what I'm saying is, I'm sorry. I swear we'll find a way for you two to spend time together. Maybe…" She paused. "Maybe you could have him for a few weeks during the summers, and over some of the holiday breaks. If you want him."

"If I want him? I never stopped wanting him, Teresa. He's my son in every way that counts. I'll always want whatever time I can have with him."

"Harry, I'm so sorry—"

"Shh. I get it now." And he did. He finally saw that Teresa had been brave enough to admit their relationship wasn't working. And it might not have been so bad if losing her hadn't meant losing Lucas. "We'll sort it out."

"Thanks. I'll call in a few days and we'll set something up. It's too late for Thanksgiving, but maybe over Christmas?"

Time at Christmas with Lucas was one of the biggest gifts he could have. "Okay. Thanks, Teresa. I can't say that enough."

They said their goodbyes and hung up.

Harry couldn't get a handle on his feelings. He'd been angry at Teresa for so long, but part of him knew that she'd been right to leave. They hadn't been happy for a long time, and he'd simply ignored that fact because he didn't want to break up the illusion he had of their family. Maybe his mother had been right about that. He'd stayed with Teresa for all the wrong reasons.

"Everything all right?" Samantha asked.

He turned and saw that he was still standing at her window, looking out onto the silent street. He came back to the couch. "I don't know."

She didn't press. Didn't ask him to say more. And soon, he couldn't seem to think of anything to say at all. He tried a very lame, "So the pageant went well."

"Yeah, it did."

Normally so comfortable in each other's company, the air now felt heavy and ominous. Thinking that made him feel ridiculous, but there it was. Something was off. He could pussyfoot around it, or he could just come out and ask. "Samantha, what's wrong?" Simple and to the point.

"When you saved Stella from falling off the stage, it was clear to me that I'm going to miss you when you're gone."

He wasn't sure that he saw the connection, but that didn't alter that he was going to miss her, as well.

"We can keep in touch…." The offer sounded half-hearted even to him.

"And yet, the reasons we shouldn't keep in touch are very much related to the reasons starting a relationship made sense. We both went into it knowing when it had to end. Coming out of a breakup, there's something comforting in that. But now, the idea of you leaving isn't so very comforting."

"I have a life in Columbus. My job and the kids I work with are waiting for me. The administration gave me a sabbatical to finish my degree." For a long time he'd tried to build his life around Teresa, but that hadn't worked. Now, he had to figure out how to rebuild a life for himself.

"I know. I'm not asking—"

"I know you're not, but Samantha, if I ever get seriously involved with another woman, it won't be one with kids." He'd said the words before, but he saw that this time they really sank in.

He nodded. "When Teresa left, it hurt, but losing Lucas was like losing a son. I'd helped raise him for seven years. She didn't just end our relationship, she severed my relationship with a boy, who for all intents and purposes, was my son. It was a double whammy. When Phillip left, you still had the kids."

"Are you saying my pain was somehow less than yours?" She sounded angry now.

That's not what he was saying. Oh, hell, he didn't know what he was saying, what he was thinking. "Do you know what it's like to lose the life you'd planned? How much that hurts?" he asked, his breath ragged

"Yes," was her quiet response.

SAMANTHA THOUGHT ABOUT THE life she'd envisioned with Phillip. Watching the kids grow up and then she and Phillip were going to travel and see the world together.

Well, her kids would still grow up and eventually move away. And she could still travel. Though on her own. Solo. The word sounded so…lonely. When that day came she didn't want to do it on her own. She didn't want this on her own. She wanted…

She let the image form in her mind, an idea that had been growing since the pageant, knowing what it was she wanted.

She wanted Harry.

She wanted him to stay in Erie. She wanted to laugh with him, to make love with him. She wanted to share her life with him.

But she'd known from the start that's not what he wanted.

She understood, but it still hurt.

And it was going to hurt more when he left.

So, she had two choices.

One, she could cut him off now.

Or, two, she could treasure this time with this man, whom she cared for, then let him go.

It wasn't really a choice.

"Harry, I understand that you have baggage. And I get not wanting to get involved, especially with someone who comes with so much baggage of her own. Listen..." She hesitated, not wanting to say the words, but knowing she had to. "We've gotten through the pageant. I want to be with you for as long as I can without recriminations, but I realize that you'll be leaving, and we'll get on with our lives separately. We'll celebrate Thanksgiving, and be thankful for the time we have."

"I just don't want to hurt you when I leave."

"I'm a big girl. And I've learned that I can be complete in and of myself. But right now, we have a couple hours to ourselves before Phillip brings the kids home. I suggest we figure out some way to fill that time."

"What do you suggest?"

She took his hand and led him toward the bedroom.

He was right, it would hurt when he left because she cared for him. No, it was more than that. It was the beginning of something so much more than that.

She loved Harry Remington.

And soon he'd leave, and she loved him enough to let him go. But at least she'd have this time to hold on to.

This time with the man she loved.

Chapter Twelve

Thanksgiving afternoon, two days later, Seton opened the front door for Harry. "Hi, Mr. Rem. Mom's in the kitchen." Harry stepped inside the foyer and inhaled a yeasty, spicy smell.

"'Bye," Seton yelled, as he darted up the stairs.

Last night, an inch of snow had fallen, leaving the city covered with that first real snow of the season. Harry took of his coat and boots, and Shane ran in. "Did you see him?"

"Who him?"

"Seton. He's it."

"Ah." Harry understood Seton's bolting now. "I may or may not have seen him. I'm Switzerland, and neutral in all games of tag."

Harry hung his coat on an empty peg as Shane shook his head, and ran down the hall.

Harry spotted Seton's head peer down from upstairs. He shot Harry a thumbs-up sign, then disappeared.

Harry made his way through the living room. Stella was cuddled on the couch, wrapped in a quilt with Ruby, Marmalade and Grunge, who shot Harry a help-me sort of look.

He opened the kitchen door and found dishes lined

up on the counter and even more piled in the sink. He was pretty sure there were more on display here than he owned. "Need some help?"

"No—" Samantha started to say, but she shook her head. "Sure. Do you mind scrubbing a few pots?"

"You've got it." Harry rolled up his sleeves and started scrubbing. "I talked to my mom this morning. She's still bent out of shape I didn't come home."

Samantha kept her head down. "I would have understood if you had."

"It's a long drive in this weather—they're saying we may get another couple inches of snow. I don't relish driving four hours in it. And I'll be home in a few days. I told her we could celebrate Thanksgiving then. That seemed to placate her." He should be looking forward to going back to Columbus, but he couldn't quite muster any enthusiasm. And it didn't have anything to do with Teresa and Lucas not being there. No, it had everything to do with not being here with Samantha and the kids.

After the pageant, when he'd told Samantha he'd never want to get serious with a woman who had kids, he knew it for the lie it was. When he'd come up with the no-dating-a-woman-with-kids rule, it had made sense. The fact that he'd be leaving was a loophole when it came to dating Samantha. He hadn't planned on falling for her.

Not just falling, he noted as he glanced at her, stirring something in a bowl. She looked hot and tired, but when Stella ran into the kitchen and asked if she could have a drink, Samantha dropped everything and got her one.

Fallen.

He'd totally gone and fallen for Samantha Williams. How could he not love her?

It wasn't something he'd been looking for, and certainly wasn't something he'd planned on, but there it was. He was madly in love with Samantha Williams and he wasn't sure how she felt about him. He thought she might learn to love him, too, if he had more time.

Time.

At first, his limited time in Erie seemed like a welcome out of a temporary relationship.

Now, he wanted more time. More time to see this tentative new love with Samantha blossom into what he thought—no, *knew*—it could be. He'd lost the life he thought he wanted, and had been determined to build a life for himself. But he realized that the life he wanted included Samantha.

An idea started to form. He scrubbed a particularly gross pot, and by the time the pot was clean, he was smiling. "Hey, Sam, I finished the dishes."

She looked up, her face flushed from the warmth of the kitchen. "Thanks. That's a big help."

"I'm going to step out back for a minute and make a phone call, okay?"

She laughed. "Sure. I've got things under control here."

"Mom?" Seton hollered. "Shane's cheating at tag."

"Want me to take care of it?" Harry asked.

She laughed. "No, I've got this wonder-mom thing down to a science. I can make a Thanksgiving dinner *and* referee out-of-control tag. I'm used to doing things on my own, Harry."

It was a gentle reminder, but one that made Harry want to blurt out his not fully fleshed-out plan. He didn't, though. Instead, he patted his pocket, making sure he had his cell.

Out in the backyard, he dialed the number. "Hey, Geri, I'm sorry to interrupt your holiday, but…"

"DINNER," SAMANTHA ANNOUNCED at three on the dot. The kids thundered into the dining room and took their seats.

Harry didn't thunder. He simply carried in the bowl of mashed potatoes, and shot her a look. An odd look.

He'd been doing that ever since he'd washed the dishes, and for the life of her, Samantha couldn't figure out what that look meant.

"Everything okay?" she asked him quietly as she trailed after him, the cranberry sauce in hand.

"Just fine," he told her. And though he was smiling, that look was still there. It seemed as if he was bursting to tell her something.

"Mom, Stella has that doll at the table," Shane tattled.

Samantha decided to try and figure out Harry's look later, and concentrated on Seton. She didn't reprimand him. She only smiled and said, "It's Thanksgiving, so I imagine it would be okay just this once if Miss Ruby stayed at the table, as long as no one tries to take her from Stella, and, Stella, you keep her away from the candle."

Stella stuck her tongue out at her brother, then turned to Samantha. "Can me and Miss Ruby say the grace?"

"Sure, sweetie."

"God, thanks for the food, and for my mom. I guess thanks for my brothers, too. And thanks for Harry. He builds good swings and reads books good, too. And he doesn't let me fall off stages. Amen."

The boys groaned in unison, and Samantha assured them it was a fine blessing, while Stella leaned over and whispered something to Ruby.

For the next hour, Samantha ate without worrying about sucking in her stomach or fitting into her jeans. She watched everyone else eat their meals, and felt a bit misty. She wasn't that type of woman. She didn't cry at

Hallmark commercials, and rarely even teared up at sad movies. Okay, *Steel Magnolias* got her, and *Terms of Endearment* when Debra Winger tells her son that it doesn't matter if he says he loves her, she knows he does, made Sam cry every time. But those were exceptions, not the rule.

She looked up at Stan. Her son. On the cusp of becoming an adult. She remembered him coming to her and telling her that Harry made her happy and he wanted that for her. She went from feeling misty to actually having tears gather in her eyes. She blinked hard and held them back, knowing she'd never be able to explain why she was crying to the kids. Or to Harry.

She glanced at him, sitting opposite of her. He spotted her watching him, and gave her another of those smiley looks.

She blinked back the tears even harder.

He was leaving, and she knew that Stan was right, Harry had made her happy. Well, she'd figure out a new way to be happy. She deserved to be happy.

"Can we be excused until dessert?" Stan asked politely. So grown up.

"Sure." Samantha managed to squeeze out the word between the tears that were clogging her throat.

"Thanks, Mom," Seton said, shoving back his chair.

"Yeah, it was good," Shane added.

Stella didn't say anything, she just grabbed Miss Ruby, who'd apparently enjoyed her meal, and hurried after her brothers. Samantha could hear the distant rumbling of a football game on television. "You can go watch the game, too," she offered Harry, hoping he'd take her up on the offer and give her a few minutes to get herself under control.

"I'd rather stay with you, if you don't mind."

What could she say to that? "I'm going to clear the table, then we can have the pie."

"Can we talk first?" he asked.

She nodded, even though she didn't want to talk. She wanted to have this holiday with Harry and not dwell on the fact that it was transient. That he was just an interim principal, and her interim lover.

"I leave in a week," he said without preamble.

She wasn't sure what to say to that, so she nodded. But her heart broke into little pieces at the thought. For some reason, a line from the pageant flitted through her mind—*Thanksgiving's a day to remember to start, saying thanks for the things that are near to our heart.*

Stella had remembered to be thankful for Harry, and Samantha was going to have to learn to be thankful for the time they'd had together. She'd known from the start she was going to have to let him go. She blinked rapidly and tried to force a smile. "I know. I'd rather not think about it today, though. I'd just like to enjoy the moment. Let's have that pie."

He took her hand. "Samantha, I don't want to go back to Columbus by myself. I don't want to rattle through my house on my own."

The boys cheered in the living room, then Stella screamed, "Seton, cut it out." There was a pause. "Mom."

Whatever Seton had done, he must have undone it because Stella called, "Never mind."

"I want this," Harry said, nodding toward the very loud noises emanating from the living room. He gave her hand a small squeeze. "I don't want to leave you, Sami. I've fallen in love with you."

Samantha didn't need to blink because his words

shook her, evaporating all her unshed tears and forcing her heart to do a double beat. "Harry, we agreed—"

"It's not what I set out to do, but it happened. I love you."

"But you said you didn't want to fall for a woman with kids."

"I'll confess, after losing Teresa and Lucas, I didn't. At least not just any woman, and not just any kids. Even as I repeated those words the other night, I realized that I had no choice in the matter. I love you…and I love your kids."

"Harry, you're leaving. In a week," she reminded him.

"Samantha, you haven't said anything I haven't thought about. What I'm hoping you'll say next is how you feel about me."

Part of her was afraid to say the words. Terrified that it would make her feelings for Harry too real. The old Samantha might have let that fear stop her, but the new one—the one who was optimistic, who knew she had a right to be happy—that Samantha blurted out, "I think I love you, too. It doesn't matter though, you're still going next week." She needed that reminder.

"I don't want to go without you."

Suddenly she understood what he'd meant when he said it hurt that Teresa hadn't even asked him to go with her. It salved some of her pain, knowing he was asking her. "Harry, if things were different, I'd follow you. If it were even last summer, I would. I'd pack up the kids and follow you anywhere. Now, Phillip's trying, and the kids deserve to know their father, to have him be a part of their lives. And I just can't—"

"Ask me," he simply said.

"What?"

"Teresa never asked me to come with her. That hurt the most," he said, echoing what she'd just been thinking.

"Would you?" Samantha asked, even as she wondered how any woman could walk away from Harry. She didn't think she could. "Would you have followed her?"

"To be honest, I think there was something missing from our relationship for a very long time, and she was honest enough to admit it. Maybe the fact that I didn't follow her anyway, without her asking, says it all. If we'd really had a love to build a life on, surely I would have. We were missing something. But Samantha, I don't think anything's missing from what we're building. I love you. So…ask me."

She was stuck on the idea that he loved her, she couldn't keep up with any other part of the conversation. "Ask you what?"

"Ask me to stay, Sami. Just ask me."

How could she do that? "Harry, I couldn't ask you to give up your life."

"Don't you see, if you let me walk away, that's what you're asking me to do. Because my life is here, with you."

He'd sat there, pouring out his heart to her from the other end of the table. Now, he got up and made his way to her. "Please, tell me you want me to stay."

"You'd stay?"

"Only if you want me to. Samantha, I tried, I really tried, to make things work with Teresa. I learned that a relationship, love, has to be a two-way street. I want to stay, but I won't, if you don't want—"

"Harry," she interrupted. "Want? You think I wouldn't want you to?"

She reached out and brushed a hand across his cheek. "I want you with me more than anything I've ever wanted. How could you doubt that?" She took a deep breath. "I love you, Harry."

He leaned in and kissed her, then pulled back, smiling. "I'm awfully glad you do, because I love you, too. I called my boss in Columbus. Already tendered my resignation right after I talked to Geri. I'll be staying on at Erie Elementary. It might have been awkward if you didn't want me to stay."

"What about that other guy?"

"He's taking another position. Erie Elementary is mine."

"That's what you were doing out in the yard?" She laughed, not that it was funny, but rather that the emotions were pressing so hard against her chest that she had to do something to relieve the pressure. "No more interim principal?"

"No more interim anything." He paused. "Samantha, part of me, a very big part, would like to ask you to marry me right now. But I think we both need more time."

Time. She'd been counting down the time she had with Harry since September. Three months hadn't seemed long enough, but now? "Now that you're staying, we have all the time in the world."

"Well, I may be gentleman enough to give you *some* time, but all the time in the world?" He shook his head. "I think you'll need to move a little faster than that."

"Mom, Grunge brought you a present, and I think Marmalade is afraid of mice," Stella hollered.

Crash.

Bang.

Crash. "Mom, hurry!" someone shouted.

She turned to Harry, laughing. "Things will never be quiet around here. You realize that?"

Harry nodded. "I'm counting on it."

Epilogue

On the first Friday in December, Samantha carried a huge box of pumpkin squares into the meeting room at Erie Elementary.

"Hi," she called out, bubbling over with happiness. "You two will never guess what happened."

"That's exactly what I said to Michelle when she came in." Carly didn't seem anywhere near as bubbly as Samantha. As a matter of fact, Carly sounded rather defeated.

Michelle nodded. "And I said it back to her. Neither of you are going to believe my holiday." Michelle shook her head in a way that didn't bode well, either.

Samantha felt a pang of guilt. Her two best friends had issues. "Talking about the Christmas Fair can wait a minute. Sounds like there's a lot going on, so who goes first?" Samantha didn't want to lead off with her positive news. When no one volunteered, she suggested, "Alphabetical order?"

"Good stuff first," Carly insisted. "And by the look of things, you're the only one with that, so you go."

Though she tried to scale back her joy, she wasn't sure she managed it as she blurted, "I'm in love."

"That's not news," Michelle and Carly said in unison. They looked at each other and laughed.

"Really, it was that obvious?" At Carly's snort, Samantha shook her head. "I wish one of you had clued me in because it was news to me. And even more importantly, Harry loves me back."

"No news there, either," Michelle told her. "Anyone looking at the two of you at the Thanksgiving Pageant knew that."

"You aren't moving to Columbus, are you? Selfishly, we don't want to lose you," Carly assured her.

"No, I'm staying." And she filled them in on the details of Harry's new post. "We're going to take it slow. We don't want to make any mistakes, still, I don't think anything about what Harry and I have could be a mistake. We fit."

She could have bubbled all night, but she knew there was something wrong with her friends. "Michelle, your turn."

Michelle's smile faded. "Remember when I said Brandon wanted to find his father?"

"And he agreed to wait until he was eighteen," Samantha said.

"Well, he lied. He went looking anyway, and he found him. I don't know what I'm going to do."

Samantha couldn't imagine finding out there was some stranger with a claim to her kids. "Oh, Michelle."

"I've talked to my lawyer, and all I can do right now is wait. The lawyer suggested we get a paternity test before I start to worry too much. So, I'm not worrying." Everything about Michelle, her expression, the sag of her shoulders, said she was worrying. She shook her head. "I can't talk about it anymore. Carly?"

Samantha was concerned about Michelle, but she

didn't know what to say to comfort her. When Carly didn't respond, Samantha's concern kicked into overdrive. She prodded her. "Carly? Your turn."

Carly sighed. "I spent Friday at the police station."

As Carly told them about being arrested, the line from the Thanksgiving Pageant poem ran through Samantha's mind again. *Thanksgiving's a day to remember to start saying thanks for the things that are near to our heart.*

Samantha studied the two women and acknowledged how much she'd come to count on them over the last few months. And how thankful she was that they were in her life.

Heidi had thrown the three of them together to work on the social committee, but Sam knew they were *held* together by something much stronger.

They were friends.

And Samantha believed whatever was coming their way—Christmas fairs, Valentine dances, nights at the police station or rediscovered fathers—they'd get through it together.

Because that's what friends did.

* * * * *

Don't miss Michelle's story in
ONCE UPON A CHRISTMAS
coming in December 2008
from American Romance!

Here's a sneak peek at
THE CEO'S CHRISTMAS PROPOSITION,
the first in USA TODAY *bestselling author*
Merline Lovelace's HOLIDAYS ABROAD *trilogy*
coming in November 2008.

American Devon McShay is about to get the
Christmas surprise of a lifetime when she meets
her new client, sexy billionaire Caleb Logan, for
the very first time.

Silhouette Desire

Available November 2008

Her breath whistled out in a sigh of relief when he exited Customs. Devon recognized him right away from the newspaper and magazine articles her friend and partner Sabrina had looked up during her frantic prep work.

Caleb John Logan, Jr. Thirty-one. Six-two. With jet-black hair, laser-blue eyes and a linebacker's shoulders under his charcoal-gray cashmere overcoat. His jaw-dropping good looks didn't score him any points with Devon. She'd learned the hard way not to trust handsome heartbreakers like Cal Logan.

But he was a client. An important one. And she was willing to give someone who'd served a hitch in the marines before earning a B.S. from the University of Oregon, an MBA from Stanford and his first million at the ripe old age of twenty-six the benefit of the doubt.

Right up until he spotted the hot-pink pashmina, that is.

Devon knew the flash of color was more visible than the sign she held up with his name on it. So she wasn't surprised when Logan picked her out of the crowd and cut in her direction. She'd just plastered on her best businesswoman smile when he whipped an arm around her waist. The next moment she was sprawled against his cashmere-covered chest.

"Hello, brown eyes."

Swooping down, he covered her mouth with his.

Sheer astonishment kept Devon rooted to the spot for a few seconds while her mind whirled chaotically. Her first thought was that her client had downed a few too many drinks during the long flight. Her second, that he'd mistaken the kind of escort and consulting services her company provided. Her third shoved everything else out of her head.

The man could kiss!

His mouth moved over hers with a skill that ignited sparks at a half dozen flash points throughout her body. Devon hadn't experienced that kind of spontaneous combustion in a while. A *long* while.

The sparks were still popping when she pushed off his chest, only now they fueled a flush of anger.

"Do you always greet women you don't know with a lip-lock, Mr. Logan?"

A smile crinkled the skin at the corners of his eyes. "As a matter of fact, I don't. That was from Don."

"Huh?"

"He said he owed you one from New Year's Eve two years ago and made me promise to deliver it."

She stared up at him in total incomprehension. Logan hooked a brow and attempted to prompt a non-existent memory.

"He abandoned you at the Waldorf. Five minutes before midnight. To deliver twins."

"I don't have a clue who or what you're..."

Understanding burst like a water balloon.

"Wait a sec. Are you talking about Sabrina's old boyfriend? Your buddy, who's now an ob-gyn doc?"

It was Logan's turn to look startled. He recovered faster than Devon had, though. His smile widened into a rueful grin.

"I take it you're not Sabrina Russo."

"No, Mr. Logan, I am *not*."

* * * * *

Be sure to look for
THE CEO'S CHRISTMAS PROPOSITION
by Merline Lovelace.
Available in November 2008 wherever books are sold,
including most bookstores, supermarkets, drugstores
and discount stores.

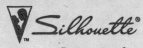

Romantic
SUSPENSE

Lindsay McKenna
Susan Grant

Mission: Christmas

Celebrate the holidays with a pair
of military heroines and their daring men
in two romantic, adventurous stories
from these bestselling authors.

Featuring:

"The Christmas Wild Bunch"
by *USA TODAY* bestselling author
Lindsay McKenna

and

"Snowbound with a Prince"
by *New York Times* bestselling author
Susan Grant

Available November wherever books are sold.

REQUEST YOUR FREE BOOKS!

2 FREE NOVELS PLUS 2
FREE GIFTS!

Love, Home & Happiness!

YES! Please send me 2 FREE Harlequin® American Romance® novels and my 2 FREE gifts (gifts are worth about $10). After receiving them, if I don't wish to receive any more books, I can return the shipping statement marked "cancel." If I don't cancel, I will receive 4 brand-new novels every month and be billed just $4.24 per book in the U.S. or $4.99 per book in Canada. That's a savings of close to 15% off the cover price! It's quite a bargain! Shipping and handling is just 25¢ per book, along with any applicable taxes.* I understand that accepting the 2 free books and gifts places me under no obligation to buy anything. I can always return a shipment and cancel at any time. Even if I never buy another book from Harlequin, the two free books and gifts are mine to keep forever.

154 HDN EEZK   354 HDN EEZV

Name	(PLEASE PRINT)	
Address		Apt. #
City	State/Prov.	Zip/Postal Code

Signature (if under 18, a parent or guardian must sign)

Mail to the **Harlequin Reader Service:**
IN U.S.A.: P.O. Box 1867, Buffalo, NY 14240-1867
IN CANADA: P.O. Box 609, Fort Erie, Ontario L2A 5X3

Not valid to current subscribers of Harlequin® American Romance® books.

Want to try two free books from another line?
Call 1-800-873-8635 or visit www.morefreebooks.com.

* Terms and prices subject to change without notice. N.Y. residents add applicable sales tax. Canadian residents will be charged applicable provincial taxes and GST. Offer not valid in Quebec. This offer is limited to one order per household. All orders subject to approval. Credit or debit balances in a customer's account(s) may be offset by any other outstanding balance owed by or to the customer. Please allow 4 to 6 weeks for delivery. Offer available while quantities last.

Your Privacy: Harlequin is committed to protecting your privacy. Our Privacy Policy is available online at www.eHarlequin.com or upon request from the Reader Service. From time to time we make our lists of customers available to reputable third parties who may have a product or service of interest to you. If you would prefer we not share your name and address, please check here. ☐

HAR08R2

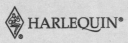

HARLEQUIN®

American ★ Romance®

LAURA MARIE ALTOM
A Daddy
for Christmas
THE STATE OF PARENTHOOD

Single mom Jesse Cummings is struggling
to run her Oklahoma ranch and raise her
two little girls after the death of her husband.
Then on Christmas Eve, a miracle strolls onto
her land in the form of tall, handsome bull
rider Gage Moore. He doesn't plan on staying,
but in the season of miracles, anything
can happen....

***Available November
wherever books are sold.***

LOVE, HOME & HAPPINESS

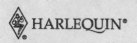

HARLEQUIN®

American ★ Romance®

COMING NEXT MONTH

#1233 A DADDY FOR CHRISTMAS by Laura Marie Altom
The State of Parenthood
Single mom Jesse Cummings is struggling to run her Oklahoma ranch and
raise her two little girls. Then a miracle strolls onto her land in the form of a
tall, handsome Texan. Gage Moore has his own troubles, so he doesn't plan on
staying. But in the season of miracles, anything can happen....

#1234 THE CHRISTMAS COWBOY by Judy Christenberry
The Lazy L Ranch
Hank Ledbetter isn't the type of cowboy to settle down and raise a family. So
when his grandfather orders him to give private riding lessons to Andrea Jacobs—
a woman so *not* his type—he's bowled over by his attraction to the New York
debutante. Andrea has another man in her life...but Hank's determined to be the
only man kissing her this Christmas!

#1235 MISTLETOE BABY by Tanya Michaels
4 Seasons in Mistletoe
Rachel and David Waide want nothing more than to have a child. But after
years of trying they are growing apart. Then Rachel discovers she is—at long
last—pregnant! Now the two have to work their way back and remember all
the love they used to share. Luckily, they'll receive a little help—in the form of
a wedding, and the magic of Christmas.

#1236 THE COWBOY AND THE ANGEL by Marin Thomas
In his cowboy gear, Duke Dalton stands out in a crowd in downtown Detroit.
He's there to set up his business, but some runaway kids are bunking in his
warehouse. They need a Christmas angel—Renée Sweeney. And though Renée
will do what she can to help the children, she wants nothing to do with Duke!

www.eHarlequin.com

HARCNM1008